Tarian Alpha

(New Tarian Pride, Book 1)

T. S. JOYCE

Tarian Alpha

ISBN: 9781797410319
Copyright © 2019, T. S. Joyce
First electronic publication: February 2019

T. S. Joyce
www.tsjoyce.com

All Rights Are Reserved. No part of this book may be used or reproduced in any manner whatsoever without written permission, except in the case of brief quotations embodied in critical articles and reviews. The unauthorized reproduction or distribution of this copyrighted work is illegal. No part of this book may be scanned, uploaded or distributed via the Internet or any other means, electronic or print, without the author's permission.

NOTE FROM THE AUTHOR:

This book is a work of fiction. The names, characters, places, and incidents are products of the writer's imagination or have been used fictitiously and are not to be construed as real. Any resemblance to persons, living or dead, actual events, locale or organizations is entirely coincidental. The author does not have any control over and does not assume any responsibility for third-party websites or their content.

Published in the United States of America

First digital publication: February 2019
First print publication: February 2019

Editing: Corinne DeMaagd
Cover Photography: Wander Aguiar
Cover Model: Josh Mario

DEDICATION

For the queens who fix the crowns of other queens.

ACKNOWLEDGMENTS

I couldn't write these books without some amazing people behind me. A huge thanks to Corinne DeMaagd, for helping me to polish my books, and for being an amazing and supportive friend. Looking back on our journey here, it makes me smile so big. You are an incredible teammate, C!

Thanks to Josh Mario, the cover model for this book. And thank you to Wander Aguiar and his amazing team for this shot for the cover. You always get the perfect image for what I'm needing.

And last but never least, thank you, awesome reader. You have done more for me and my stories than I can even explain on this teeny page. You found my books, and ran with them, and every share, review, and comment makes release days so incredibly special to me.

1010 is magic and so are you.

ONE

Ronin Alder couldn't stop staring at the creature his best friend had turned into.

Grim was dominant, good at fighting, and being groomed to take over the Tarian Pride someday, but this…this…monster didn't belong inside of Ronin's friend.

The lion pacing the incineration room had a pitch-black mane and bore the red angry scars of the fight. His eyes were gold instead of green, and when the lion saw Ronin looking through the small window, he roared and charged. There was no recognition in the animal's face as he slammed into the metal door over and over. Ronin knew that if there was no barrier between them, the lion would kill him.

The council called him the Reaper.

Ronin had watched his best friend die in a dominance fight with Justin Moore. He'd died. Everyone had seen it. The entire Pride had watched him bleed out, and none of the council would let Ronin or Grim's grandmother, Rose, try to save him. All Ronin had been able to do was watch Grim's final breaths and drag Rose against him so she could fall apart.

The sound of breaking bones echoed through the incineration room. Two days ago, Grim's body had been put in here and covered with a sheet to burn. But then the council had found him Changed into this—the Reaper.

A groan of agony sounded. "Ronin," Grim rasped out. He had to be delirious with pain. He'd been Changing every few minutes for days. "Ronin, please."

"Please what?" Ronin asked.

"Kill me."

Ronin turned suddenly and slammed his back against the door, then slid down to the floor and buried his face in his hands. Sixteen years old, and he knew what he had to do. He owed it to Grim to save him from this hell.

"Who will I have if you leave?" Ronin asked thickly.

"Rose." Grim almost choked on the word. The Reaper was growling again already. *"Take care of my grandma."*

"But..." Ronin swallowed hard and tried to imagine his life without Grim. He didn't have parents. He didn't make friends, didn't attach to people. He'd known Grim was his to protect from the time he was a cub. How many nights had he spent with Rose and Grim, his make-shift family, and now he would be called upon to murder half of it? He would just as soon cut out his own heart.

It wasn't fair.

"Ronin," Grim snarled out in a voice he didn't even recognize. *"Please."*

A tear slid down Ronin's cheek as he pulled the long blade from the sheath at his belt. When he Changed back to his human form, Ronin would have to make it quick. Blade to the neck. He would hold him close so Grim would know he wasn't alone at the end. Not like in that killing field where this creature was born.

The door behind him rattled with the force of the Reaper slamming against it.

"I know what you're planning," Leon said as he

stepped from the shadows down the hall.

Ronin startled hard, nicking his thumb on the blade where he'd been checking the sharpness. He hadn't realized anyone was here.

"The council has plans for him," Leon said above the roaring that rattled the walls.

"You always had plans for him, and look what happened. Look what you did."

"It's a miracle," Leon said, his eyes in the deep shadows cast by the single hanging lightbulb in the short, narrow hallway that separated them. The harsh lighting made him look like a corpse. Leon approached slowly as he spoke. "The Tarian Pride has been getting too soft lately. There are too many submissives. We need to cull some, and the people here are forgetting how important the culls are. They keep us strong. We needed a sign, a weapon, and…the Reaper landed in our laps."

"Fuck you, Leon. He's only eighteen. He's a kid, and you ruined his entire life by forcing that monster out of him. One lion inside of him wasn't enough? You think it's some sort of blessing that he has two? I wish it was you lying in that field bleeding out. Someday it will be, and I'll be holding the knife in your gut. I swear it."

The roaring of the Reaper was deafening as Leon approached him. From the other side of the hallway, two more council members stalked toward Ronin.

Ronin huffed a laugh and stood. Weak, weak, weak. The council had this stupid notion that only dominants were important, but look at these three dominants. Three mature males on one sixteen-year-old kid. He gripped the handle of the knife and glared at the council members with all the hatred that had consumed him since the Reaper had been born. They didn't understand that their "weapon" couldn't be tamed or controlled. The animal roaring to be released was a murder machine, plain and simple. It had killed the good parts of his friend. The Reaper had killed Grim. The council, with their need for war had killed Grim.

So fuck it.

Realization filled Leon's glowing gold eyes in the second Ronin reached for the door handle to release the Reaper. It was the first time Ronin had ever seen fear there.

Ronin offered the three lion shifters sprinting toward him an empty smile. "It's the council that needs to be culled."

And then he yanked open the door.

"Ronin!"

With a gasp, Ronin shot up in bed.

Kannon was standing in the doorway, eyes wide and gold. It was just Kannon here, not the council. The council was long dead. It had been just a dream. A nightmare. Ronin was here in the big house in Tarian Pride Territory again after all these years. That's why the damn dream had returned. That's why the memories were haunting him again.

"What's happened?" he snarled.

Kannon ran his hand though his black hair and swallowed hard. "Rose is gone."

"Gone?"

"Yeah, she's not in her house."

Ronin forced his muscles to relax. God, he was drenched in sweat. "Well, she's a grown woman, Kannon. She's entitled to spend her nights wherever she wants."

"Understood, but…"

"But what?" Ronin snapped.

Kannon swallowed hard. "It looks like there was a struggle. We found blood. It smells like it belongs to

Rose. Do you want me to call the Reaper?"

She'd been taken, and he knew exactly who took her. Fury seared through Ronin's words as he murmured, "No. I'll handle it."

TWO

Today was the worst day of Emerald Lawson's life.

It should've been the happiest. Engaged. Paired up. On the eve of the day most girls have dreamed of since childhood.

In the back seat of the SUV, she stared at the woods blurring by to avoid looking at the stranger who would walk her down the aisle.

Derek was her age, and he was Tarian through and through. She didn't mean that in a good way. She *hated* the Tarian Pride. Her parents had run years ago, and Emerald had been lucky enough to be raised rogue. Just her, Mom, and Dad.

Mom had passed away a few years back, and the

Tarian Pride council had been killed off in a stupid war they'd started. The Pride split, New Tarian and Old Tarian. It was the Old Tarian half that had come sniffing around last year. Bullying her and Dad. Scaring them. She'd moved cities twice in one year, and Derek and the others had still found her both times.

Why did they care?

Bloodlines.

Fuckin' bloodlines. Her lineage traced back to one of the founding families of the Tarian Pride and in a time of rebuilding, that apparently counted for a whole lot.

"Everything looks good. Your handwriting is shit, though. I can barely read your signature on the contract," Derek murmured amid the sound of paper rustling.

It had ripped her soul out to sign it. She wasn't sorry that she'd scribbled. If he looked close enough, it said *fuck you* in the middle of all of her signatures.

She hated, hated, hated the Tarian Pride.

And now she would be Queen.

How had she found herself here, speeding toward her internal death? She glanced forward, checked the speed. Going sixty-five miles an hour up winding, mountain roads. Sixty-five miles an hour toward the end of the happy part of her life.

For the dozenth time, Annamora glanced at her in the rearview. There was always worry sitting in the too-bright gold hue of her lion shifter eyes. "It'll be okay."

"Annamora," Derek snarled, "Cassius doesn't pay you to have an opinion."

"He doesn't pay me at all," Annamora whispered.

Oh, no.

Derek lurched forward and grabbed Annamora's throat so fast, he blurred. "The fuck did you say to me?"

The SUV swerved, and Annamora hit the brakes hard, choking loudly.

"Let her go!" Emerald yelled as the rig rocked to a stop on the shoulder.

Derek ignored her and yanked Annamora back against the seat. He hissed into her ear, "You fuckin' slut. You remember your place, you submissive piece of shit. Or do you need me to remind you?"

Why couldn't she move? Why couldn't Emerald hit him? Her fists were clenched but stayed helpless on the tops of her thighs. Heat boiled through her, but she couldn't even lift her gaze from the floorboard.

All the memories of her time with the Tarian Pride as a cub flooded back. *Submissive piece of shit.*

Annamora and Emerald were the same. They had no value to the dominant-heavy Old Tarian Pride. No value but their lineage.

Submissives were worthless.

She wanted to hit him. Annamora was gasping for air as Derek murmured vile insults into her ear. For what? For telling Emerald everything would be okay? For offering her comfort? *Hit him.*

But as always around dominants, her inner lioness crouched, got smaller and more terrified until Emerald couldn't feel the big cat inside of her at all.

Worthless.

She hadn't felt this low in years.

Hit him!

Her nails dug into her palms, but still, she couldn't throw the punch. Emerald slammed her head back, trying to shake her mind loose from the control this undeserving dominant had over her animal. Shitty Tarian males. They were all like Derek. When she was a cub, all the males were one big blur except for Dad. Dad and a boy. A boy she'd watched as a little girl. Blond hair, blue eyes that turned to a striking green-gold when his lion got riled up. He was dominant, but showed kindness. And that kindness had gotten him killed. Ronin. Emerald tried to hide in the good memory of the boy who had stopped another kid from hurting her on the playground. Nice cub. Orphan. Hard life, but he'd still been nice when he was alive. People could be nice.

Remember...people can be nice. Don't let them break you. Don't let them make you bitter. Don't let them make you forget that people can be good.

When Derek slammed Annamora's head against the headrest, Emerald jumped, jolted from the memory. Tears of anger streamed down Emerald's cheeks as she sat frozen.

Derek sat back next to her and began going through the contract again, as if he hadn't just hurt a woman.

She wanted to puke. The worst part? Annamora wasn't even crying, didn't even rub her neck, didn't show pain. Emerald witnessed the exact moment Annamora shut down. In the rearview mirror, Emerald could see the fear fade from her eyes, and then Annamora's expression went blank. Her breathing steadied out. She didn't show any emotion at all. She just put the SUV back into gear and began driving again.

That's what Tarian dominants did to submissive females. They broke them.

Annamora was Emerald's future.

But what choice did she have other than to sign her life away and marry Cassius, the new Alpha of the Old Tarian Pride?

He had taken her father.

Emerald recognized the road when Annamora edged the SUV around the curve of a cliff. It tugged at some long-buried memory of this place. She hadn't been back to Telluride, Colorado since Mom and Dad had run away with her in the night. She'd only been fourteen years old. Fifteen years, and she'd tried to think about this place as little as possible. And now here she was again, about to tether herself to these mountains for always.

On either side of the two-lane road, massive mountains jutted up toward the sky, covered in snow and pine trees. A green sign on the side of the road read *Telluride city limit, ELEV 8750 FT*. She was going to have to get used to the dryer climate and thinner air. It was the end of January and freezing outside. A thin layer of ice covered the road as Annamora drove them straight through the quaint town. Population 2,300 or so from the Wikipedia page she'd looked up about it as she waited for Derek and Annamora to collect her and the one sad suitcase from in front of the house she'd rented in Sterling, Colorado for the last year.

She didn't even want to think about the life she'd left behind. It would only make this harder.

She checked the cell phone that had been sitting facedown next to her. Her dad's smiling face lit up the lock screen, her reminder not to jump out of this damn car and make a run for it. If she paired up with Cassius tomorrow, the Old Tarian Pride would set him free. It was in the contract. If she didn't, they would kill him. Simple as that. And they wouldn't lose a single ounce of sleep because that was what the Tarian Pride did. They killed and bullied and took. No wonder all the other shifter Crews hated them. It was a Pride full of monsters that had bred monsters who bred monsters for generations until evil was ingrained in their DNA.

"Control your emotions, or I'll have to put you in your place, Queen," Derek said in a soft, low, dangerous voice.

She hadn't realized she was growling. She swallowed the sound down and turned the phone off so the picture of her smiling dad wouldn't see her expose her neck and lower her gaze for a man like Derek.

And there was Annamora's dead eyes in the rearview mirror, checking on her again. Annamora didn't know it, but she was probably Emerald's best friend in the world right now.

They drifted straight through town and another twenty minutes into the mountains, right along the edge of the Rio Grand National Forest. 1.8 million acres of wilderness and the perfect place for a Pride of monstrous lions to get away with murder. Which they probably had infinite times.

Everything would be fine. Dad wouldn't be one of their numbers. She'd signed the contract and so had Cassius.

It wasn't fair. *Stop!* She couldn't think like that. She couldn't get angry. She'd already torn her rental house to shreds in her fury when she'd found out they'd taken him. She'd dealt with the anger. Mostly. Now she just needed to make sure he was released safely. Tarians were no shifters to mess around with. Everyone knew they didn't bluff.

These mountains were stunning—this place would be soooo beautiful if she hadn't attached it to every bad memory from her childhood.

Except for her parents. And Ronin, the nice boy.

There were still nice people.

Annamora parked the SUV in a white gravel parking lot with woods surrounding it. On the other side was a bridge, not one of those sturdy ones, but a hanging bridge. Well, this part she didn't remember.

"What happened to the Tarian Pride Territory?" she asked Annamora as they all got out.

Annamora blinked slowly and looked at her with a vacant expression. There were red marks on her neck in the shape of Derek's fingers. "You want help with your suitcase?" Annamora asked.

Emerald swallowed hard and shook her head. "I can get it."

"Let's go," Derek barked out. "Cassius will be eager to meet you." He strode toward the bridge, contract flapping in the frigid breeze in his hand.

She wished she could burn the damned thing, and the man holding it while she was at it.

Tired of glaring at his wide shoulders, she made her way to the back of the SUV and pulled out her heavy suitcase. She dragged the thing behind her like a dead body. Why? Because she wasn't exactly rolling in the dough, and she'd had the damn thing since she was sixteen. Both wheels had broken off long ago. So she looked real graceful as she lugged the suitcase behind her across the stupid swinging bridge. Good thing she wasn't afraid of heights because midway through the journey to BFE, the bridge got to swaying in the wind, and she was tossed from side-to-side with nothing but air underneath her and a river with jagged rocks for a bank far, far below.

"Hurry up!" Derek yelled from the other side, his voice echoing through the valley. He was still only carrying the contract, so of course it was real easy for him to scamper across the bridge of death.

"Asshole," she muttered under her breath as she used her lioness strength to hoist the suitcase to her hip and stumble across the rest of the bridge like a drunken pinball.

She hoped her contract gave him a papercut.

Behind her, Annamora's chestnut-colored hair whipped in the wind, but the woman didn't even try to move it out of her face. She just walked like the bridge didn't affect her at all. But when the breeze blew her hair away, Emerald saw the single tear that dampened her cheek. It glistened in the light from the sunset. The woman wiped it away quick as a flash before glancing at Derek and then back down at her feet as she walked.

Sometimes Emerald thought the submissives were the toughest kind of people.

She knew that the title Queen of the Tarian Pride meant nothing because she was female, but in this moment, she swore to herself she would figure out a way to repay Annamora for her kind words in the car and make her life better, if even just a little bit.

Emerald's black hair probably looked like a bird's nest by the time they made their way up to the porch of a large cabin. Her cheeks were definitely red on account of all the fury she still had coursing through her veins, and she was beginning to sweat. She hadn't been nervous to meet Cassius until now. In fact, she hadn't thought about him much at all. Sure, she'd looked up his picture on the shifter registration site online, but he just looked like a man. A big muscleman with a shaved head and a big scar running down one side, right through his eye. She hadn't even been able to tell his eye color in the picture on the government site. He was a dominant enforcer the Old Tarians had brought in to try to revive the council with all Tarian members. Ha. If they succeeded, the council would have all lion prides ruined in a year, tops.

Wise shifters didn't put monsters on thrones. The Tarian Pride had never figured that little gem out, though.

Okay, she could do this.

Derek reached for the door handle.

Maybe Cassius would be a fair mate. Not a love-match, but perhaps he wouldn't be as bad as she'd feared. Maybe he would like her and protect her, listen to her and—

"Where the fuck is my stew?" came a bellowing demand from inside.

Derek gave her an empty smile. "Your mate." And then he shoved open the door.

There was a sprawling dining table right in the middle of the great room, and at the head of it sat

Cassius. He slammed his fist on the table. "Sora, I swear to God, if I don't have that bowl in front of me in five seconds, I'm going to beat your ass."

The Sora in question was a platinum blond-haired, mouse of a woman who was standing in the kitchen on the other side, ladling stew into a bowl as fast as her shaking hands could work.

"Fuck!" Cassius yelled, startling the two brunettes sitting on either side of him. Twins? "I hate training new ones."

"By training, he means beating," Derek murmured. He was definitely trying to scare Emerald, and it was definitely working.

"Come here!" Cassius yelled.

"Coming," Sora whispered, speed-walking toward him, her neck exposed.

"I wasn't talking to you, bitch." Cassius dragged his attention to Emerald. "I was talking to you." He clasped his hands in front of his chiseled jaw and arched one dark eyebrow. His eyes blazed a brighter gold as he looked her up and down, pausing on her curves.

Emerald wanted to retch. She'd never had a man look straight through her before, like she was nothing. Like she was a ghost.

"Little thicker than I like." He twitched his head. "Perky tits, though. Hair needs to be dyed. I don't like black hair." He leaned back in the creaking chair and stretched one leg out as he narrowed his gaze at her. "Those eyes, though. I heard about your eyes. That's where you got your name, right? Because they're so green."

"Actually—"

"I don't care," he cut her off. He snapped his finger and held out his hand, and like a little sewer rat, Derek started to scramble toward his Alpha.

Before she could change her mind, Emerald lurched forward, reached out, and yanked the contract from Derek's hand. She held it up, threatening to rip it down the middle. "I want to see my father first."

Fury flashed across Cassius's face, and he stood. And stood. And stood. Good God, the man was tall as a mountain and built like a brick house.

Derek laughed and muttered, "Oh, she has a death wish."

The females were all frozen with their heads down, even Sora, who had skidded to a stop and was staring at the bowl of steaming stew, chest heaving.

Emerald tried to hold Cassius's gaze. Truly, she did. She tried harder than she'd ever tried at anything in her life, but inside, her lioness was panicking, and she had to lower her eyes. Emerald's entire body started shaking as he approached her slowly. She focused on his thick-soled boots, clomping closer and closer. The floorboards didn't even dare to creak under his weight.

"Did you just come into my den and demand something of me?" he asked.

"Y-yes."

"Without the stutter, bitch."

Emerald inhaled deeply and nodded as she said, "Yes." Her stupid voice cracked on the word, though.

Cassius grabbed her lower jaw and yanked her face up toward his. "If I didn't want you lookin' pretty for tomorrow, I would beat that demand right out of your fuckin' face." His voice held such terrifying conviction, she had no doubt he wanted to hurt her. His grip tightened on her jaw. It hurt, and she flinched. At her reaction, he grabbed her harder and then slammed his lips against hers. All she could feel was searing pain for the one second he kissed her.

When she pushed off him and threw the contract at his face, the back of his hand hit her so hard and so fast, she was slammed down onto her knees.

Stars orbited her peripheral vision, and there was a loud roaring sound in her ears along with a high-pitched ringing. Someone was yelling. Yelling? She couldn't make out any words. Her head was ripped back, the hand in the back of her hair too rough, and Cassius glared down at her, turning her face from side to side. "Tell them to only photograph her from the left side tomorrow," he snarled. And then he released her and strode toward Sora. He yanked the bowl of food from her hands and yelled, "Everyone get the fuck out!"

The women all jogged out the front door, heads lowered, but they all blurred together because Emerald still couldn't see straight. Her face hurt so bad. She'd never been struck before, and perhaps she was in shock.

Gentle hands were pulling her, tugging her toward the door. Annamora? Emerald wanted to help, but she reached for her suitcase.

"We'll get it later," Annamora whispered as quiet as a breath.

Derek was outside already by the time Emerald and Annamora hit the front porch. He was talking to a group of men, a dozen at least, all huge and muscled with glowing eyes and snarls on their faces. They all looked different and the same at once.

"Is that her?" one of them asked. "The new mate? Is that her?"

"The new mate?" Emerald murmured.

"There are four of you," Annamora whispered from behind her. Was she hiding behind Emerald?

Oh my gosh, oh my gosh, oh my gosh. She wasn't the only mate? What the fucking fuck?

"She has the look of the Lawsons," one of them said, scratching the dark beard on his jaw. "But she feels submissive as fuck. Why does Cassius keep pairing up with submissives?"

Uh, because breaking submissive women fuels his gigantic ego? Idiots! She wasn't even a psych major, but that much was plain and obvious after spending two minutes with their Alpha. That man was seriously messed up.

"Her face is already bleeding," another said low to Derek. "Is she one of them willful ones?" Why did he look hungry when he asked that?

"If..." Emerald clenched her hands at her sides to calm her nerves. And then she wiped her bleeding lip, smearing red across the back of her knuckles. "If you'll excuse me, I've had a long day of travel and would like to clean up before I properly introduce myself to everyone." And then like she was in a dream, she floated down the stairs and through the grumbling crowd toward the woods. She didn't have one freaking clue where she was going, only that she had to get away from everyone so she could properly fall apart.

Cassius had hit her.

He'd really hit her.

She'd never felt more degraded and disgusted in all her life. Her cheek had a pulse, and her split lip hurt so bad. The tears were falling out of her eyes and she couldn't even stop them if she tried.

"This way," Annamora said, grabbing her hand.

Emerald just held it like a kid going to her first day of kindergarten because, truth-be-told, she was hurt and scared and her lioness liked affection and comfort. Always had.

"It'll be better when you learn the rules," Annamora whispered in a heartbroken voice. "If you can learn to anticipate his needs…or I don't know…" The woman's shoulders sagged. "I didn't want Derek to find you. I wanted you to stay far away."

"What?"

"Well…don't you remember me?"

Emerald stopped and turned to Annamora. "I know you?"

"We're the same age. So…we did homeschool together for a couple years. There were a bunch of us, but I always remembered you. You were nice to everyone, even when the boys were mean to you. I think you'll stay nice. All the females here are trying to stay nice, too. I'm sorry," she blurted out, grabbing Emerald's hands. "I thought you really got away, then I was the one who drove you back here."

"Did you have a choice?" Emerald asked.

Annamora shook her head. They just told me to drive to pick someone up. I didn't know it was you. I think you could've knocked me over with a feather when I saw it was you sitting on that curb with your suitcase. I wish it was anyone else. No, it wasn't my choice to bring you back here. Not at all."

"Then don't waste another second on guilt for something that isn't your fault."

"Oh, Talon Lawson! Your dad!" Annamora whispered, tugging her toward a long row of small, identical, one room, quick-build cabins. "He's okay. He's in one of the small cabins back in the woods, him and this other lady Cassius just brought in last night. I just don't know which cabins they have them stashed in, so we'll have to look around a little. Rose, the woman Cassius kidnapped used to be one of us, but she sided with the New Tarian Pride when we all split. She was the only female who escaped. But Cassius brought her back. If you want to see your dad, now is the time. The boys are still back at the big house and Cassius's mates will be headed to shower while they can. He keeps them close most of the time. The other females are all down by the creek doing laundry. The pipes froze up here a few days ago so there isn't water for the washing machines right now. Come on. It's gettin' dark, so we won't be seen as easy. We have to be quick, though, and you have to keep it together. Promise me. No going to pieces and trying to escape with your dad. Cassius would catch you. He's the best hunter I've ever known. He's scary good, him and Derek." Annamora tugged her off to the side, behind the row of cabins and straight into the brush.

"Why are you doing this?" Emerald whispered, remembering the punishment Annamora had taken the last time she'd offered comfort.

"Because you got hit. And the way you acted...you ain't never been hit before. But maybe seeing your dad will take some of the sadness out of your eyes."

"And if you get caught?" Emerald asked.

Annamora sighed and shrugged. "I get in trouble all the time. At least this one will be worth it."

And that was the mark of a good woman. Someone who knew the consequences of doing a good deed, but did it anyway.

The woods seemed to get darker by the second. The sun had disappeared behind the mountains, and now Emerald could barely see where she was walking. She had good night vision, but the forest was thick and full of shadows. Annamora picked her way right through like a sure-footed billy goat, but Emerald tripped time and time again over the knotty roots and brush reaching for her ankles. It was like skeleton hands reaching up from a graveyard to pull her under, and here she went again with her imagination running wild. She didn't much like the dark, and neither did her lioness.

A few minutes into their hike, and she couldn't even see the lights from the rows of cabins behind them anymore. Her face hurt, so did her pride and, truth-be-told, her heart was breaking a little. Everything had been going wrong for a while. She just couldn't believe she was here, in the Old Tarian Pride camp, bound by a contract to an awful man who would hurt her again the first chance he got.

The tears were warm on her cheeks, and they angered her. Weak. She always did this, had a chance to be strong and cried instead. All these stupid emotions that were always roiling around in her like little tornadoes. She didn't really want to see Dad with tear stains on her cheeks and a swollen face and fat lip.

And just as she was about to ask how much farther, there was a commotion up ahead. Rustling. Loud rustling and a grunt. There was a light through the woods, appearing and disappearing as Emerald moved through the trees, but Annamora had started jogging toward the sound, high-kneeing it like she couldn't wait to meet the scary sound.

No, no, no! A wise woman did not run toward

danger!

"Annamora!" Emerald called but her new friend was gone.

Heart hammering out of her chest, Emerald tried to catch up to her, but tripped right on the edge of the clearing. There was a tiny cabin where a man was beating the everlovin' shit out of another man on the ground. Just...pummeling him with a closed fist over and over. It was dark and the man was cast in deep shadows, but there was something familiar about him. Something about his face...

"We're being attacked," Annamora said under her breath, appearing suddenly behind Emerald. "That's not one of ours. That's the Alpha of the New Tarian Pride."

"But...my dad..." Emerald said in a stunned voice, unable to take her eyes off the scuffle. That Alpha was going to kill the man with his bare hands. She'd never seen such raw violence before today.

Annamora yanked on her shirt, but Emerald just stood there on the edge of the porchlight, frozen in equal parts awe and horror.

The Alpha of the New Tarian Pride was a killer.

"Girl, you're on your own. I have to warn

everyone," Annamora said on a shaking breath, and then she was off into the woods like a bullet.

Wait, what? Emerald turned and bolted for Annamora's bouncing shadow, but the farther she got from the porch light of the little cabin, the worse the visibility became. She sniffed the air, but there had been a lot of shifters in these woods so everything was mixed up and confusing. This way. No...this way. Emerald skidded to a stop, huffing breath and looking left and right. "Annamora?" she whispered to no answer.

Oh crap, oh crap, oh crap! She was afraid of the dark, and now she was in these unfamiliar woods that belonged to monsters with a murderous rival Alpha, and probably his whole Pride was here to kill off everyone, and she was lost! She was the worst at survival ever.

Something rustled to her left, and she froze.

A lion roared suddenly in the distance, and with a squeak, Emerald ducked down and covered her ears. Woods. Dark woods. Woods with lions in them, just like the night Mom and Dad had fled the Tarian Pride. Just like then. Her face was throbbing with pain. Tears of anger and fear over those stupid memories were staining her cheeks and everything was wrong.

More rustling, closer, and she couldn't hold it back anymore. All the horror of the last year hiding from the Tarian Pride, all the anger when she'd found her dad missing, all the anguish at leaving and signing her life away. the pain in her face and her heart...

She inhaled deeply and screamed.

A hand clamped over her mouth and yanked her back against a solid wall. No, not a solid wall. Nostrils flaring, she inhaled the scent of him. Cologne, man, blood. Something musky. Masculine shampoo? Or beard oil?

The blood was the biggest scent, though. It clung to the lining of her nose and made her want to gag.

"Shhhhh," he murmured in a deep rumbling voice against her ear.

She couldn't breathe. Couldn't breathe! Her chest was going to explode as she panted for breath that didn't feed her lungs. She was panicking. Trapped. And inside, her lioness sat frozen, just like she always did around dominants, and this man was the most dominant she'd ever felt.

She was going to die. Killer. He was a killer. Couldn't breathe. She looked up to the stars, twinkling through the branches of the winter-bare trees above her.

I'm so sorry, Dad.

And then her vision collapsed inward, and everything went dark.

THREE

Shit! The girl had passed out!

She'd just gone totally limp in his arms. He clung to her, holding her close to his pounding heart as he tracked the trio of Old Tarians racing through the woods a hundred yards off. They appeared and disappeared in the trees, holding flashlights, headed right for the cabin. They wouldn't find Rose there, though, since she was crouched behind him with her hand resting on his lower back. All they would find was the carcass of the asshole who'd beat on Rose.

"Ronin," Rose whispered, sidling around him, "look at her face."

Ronin had great night vision, the only gift his good-for-nothing dad had ever given him through genetics. The moon cast her face in blue hues as he cradled her body like a child and looked upon the damage someone had done to her. She looked like Rose. He was going to fucking kill every male here. Blood was dried on her swollen lip, and her cheeks were still damp with tears. The left side of her face was so swollen it was hard to tell what she looked like.

What the fuck was he supposed to do with this? He'd only meant to keep her from screaming and giving their position away.

"We have to move," Rose whispered.

He fucking knew. He'd come here with no backup, trying to steal Rose back quietly, but he'd lost it on that lion who'd hurt her and wasted too much time.

But he sat here frozen, looking at the woman in his arms, unable to move, unable to set her down gently in the snow and leave her to endure whatever this Pride had been doing to her.

Women were queens. Queens. Male lions had it all wrong. The boys weren't important. They were weapons, but females were the intelligence. The ones who softened hard hearts and made boys salvageable.

This one had been mistreated, and he couldn't just leave her.

She'd been crying.

"Ronin," Rose warned.

Fuck. He was kidnapping two lionesses from the Old Tarian Pride tonight.

Without a word, he stood, hoisting the woman in his arms. Rose's hand stayed right on his back. She didn't see as well in the dark anymore.

He cut straight for the ravine because the Pride wouldn't expect their escape to be the hardest route. But Ronin wasn't scared of hard. Nothing in his life, and he meant *nothing*, had been easy.

And if they caught up to them, okay. He would let the snarling lion inside of him loose on this asshole Pride and see who survived. Because right now, he was in the presence of two battered women at their hands, and he was ready to steal every last one of their breaths.

If it had been only him, he would have turned back around and been a live grenade right in the heart of the Old Tarian Pride. The only thing that kept him moving forward were the tear stains on the woman's cheeks.

Someday very soon, he would have his revenge, but not tonight.

FOUR

The hazy murmur of voices dragged Emerald from a deep sleep. Perhaps she was still dreaming. So many vivid images had bombarded her slumber, but she hadn't been able to wake up. She'd had to get through them all instead. Maybe this was another one.

"...you can't just go out on your own, Alpha..."

"Kannon, how many times have I told you, stop calling me that."

"Doesn't matter how much you tell us. We're still Tarian! That's the way we talk to an Alpha."

No answer.

Kannon's voice came again. "Meeting is in ten minutes, and how are you going to explain last night?"

"I don't have to explain shit."

"Yeah, you do. You put this all together. You want to rehab us? Well then remind us why we are backing you."

"I brought Rose back—"

"Alone! Without anyone knowing! What would've happened if you got caught? If you and Rose were killed? We would have no leadership, and we would all be sitting ducks. And now you've brought *her* back here? You're going to turn this war into a fight over females, and it takes away from everything we're trying to accomplish."

A terrifying snarl rattled the air around her.

Okay, this dream wasn't that good. It was kind of scary and didn't make any sense. Emerald squinted her eyes open. The room was blurry for a moment before she focused on a tall, lean man slamming another dark-haired man against the wall.

The man against the wall exposed his throat, but his face said he wasn't sorry for anything he'd said. "I'm on your team, you know," the dark-haired man, Kannon, growled. "Not all Tarians are bad."

"Fuck!" the tall man yelled. He shoved off the

other man and sat heavily into a chair on the other side of the room. Kannon left, slamming the door behind him.

Uh, this was not a dream. Where the hell was she? Scared into stillness, she watched the man run his hands down his beard and then rest his elbows on his knees. He stared at the ground, shaking his head. In a ragged whisper, he said, "What am I doing?"

The man had blond hair, longer so it curled right at his shoulders, pushed back like he'd run his hands through it over and over. He had a thick beard, a couple shades darker, and his torso was covered in tattoos. How could she tell? Because the man wasn't wearing a shirt. A bandage was slung across his body from ribs to shoulder, and at his shoulder, there was a big blood stain, but he wasn't favoring the injury. It was definitely the man from last night, the one that had something familiar about him. She couldn't put her finger on it. It was something in his profile when he looked out the window. Sharp cheek bones, and his eyes were slightly slanted upward, giving him a feline look even in his human form. He wore dark jeans that were ripped at one knee, and a gold chain wallet sat in his back pocket, the gold chain clinking against the chair when he moved.

He didn't look so dangerous right now as he rested his chin on his clasped hands and stared out the window.

He looked...vulnerable.

She released the breath she was holding as slowly as she could, but the man snapped his attention to her. And the second they locked eyes, she was stunned into stillness again.

She knew him. Oh, God, she *knew* him. Those eyes. Those shocked, wide eyes. Blue like the ocean. They would turn goldish-green when he Changed. She'd only seen eyes like that once, in a blond little boy who had protected her on the playground when she was a cub.

"Emerald," he murmured, unblinking.

"Ronin?"

He stood and strode toward her. Three banging steps from his boots, and he stopped. His face was unreadable as he stared at her. He gestured to her face. "What happened?"

Her head hurt so much to move, but she sat up, using the covers as a shield for her body. She dragged her fingertips to her throbbing cheek. "I'm not healing very fast," she said, dropping her gaze in shame.

"That'll happen when you're stressed. Your lioness…she's…"

"She's what?"

"Shut down. I can't even feel her."

"Me either. It's her move. She leaves easy." Why did she feel like crying again? She forced the words past her tightening vocal chords. "I thought you were dead."

"Ha." He inhaled deeply and made his way to the wall, as far away from her as he could, and leaned against it. "The council tried. Damn-near succeeded too, but I had a hero."

"Who?"

"Damon Daye. A couple of the council members took me into the woods to kill me, but he was there. He and a grizzly shifter named Beaston. The griz said Damon didn't even need to kill the men wanting to slit my throat. Beaston said they had a worse fate coming, and he smiled. Leon was killed in that war against Beast last year. He lived bad, and died bad. He was killed running away, and he suffered, and when I found that out, I could just see Beaston's smile in my head. That old wily grizzly didn't have to kill Leon, didn't have to carry that death on his soul. Karma got him. That night in these woods, all those years ago, he and Damon saved me and drove me straight from Tarian territory to a Clan of tiger shifters. They plucked me from death and set me on a totally different road. One that lead me here. Those tigers turned everything around for me."

Emerald's attention dipped to his stomach. It was a tattoo of a tiger and a snake fighting. "Is that why you got that one?"

The corner of Ronin's mouth curved up into a wicked grin. "I would never get a lion."

She couldn't blame him.

"I'm glad…" She chickened out and cleared her throat. *Just say it.* "I'm glad you had heroes."

He canted his head and studied her, a slight frown lowering his blond eyebrows. "What are you doing with Old Tarian?"

All of her heartbreak flooded her in an instant.

"I have to go back. I know where I am. I've seen this room before."

"It's my room."

She swallowed hard. "It's the Alpha's room in the

big house. I'm not where I'm supposed to be."

"Where are you supposed to be?"

"I signed a contract—"

"*Where*, Emerald?" he gritted out.

"At the right hand of Cassius."

"Ffffuck!" he yelled, turning away from her. "Who hit you?" he asked suddenly, fury turning his eyes that striking gold-green color.

She shook her head, trying not to think about yesterday.

"*Who*?" he asked louder.

She lifted her chin and forced herself to look him in the eyes. "Cassius has my father."

"What?" he asked, moving for her. He sat on the edge of the bed. "What do you mean?"

"I'm contracted to be Cassius's mate so he'll release my father."

Ronin's face twisted into something animal before he ripped his gaze away from her and gave her his back. There was a knock on the door. "Yes?" Ronin asked in a low, steady voice.

"Meeting, Alpha."

Ronin sighed. "Bring me Rose."

"Yes, Alpha." The echoing sound of footsteps

followed his retreat.

Ronin shook his head, his shoulders tense.

"You're alive and you're Alpha of the Tarian Pride now. I never saw that coming."

"Not the Tarian Pride." He looked to the side, giving her his profile. "The New Tarian Pride."

He was so handsome in the early morning light that filtered through the window. There was a big sunray hitting him, dust motes swirling in the air in front of his face, his crystal blue eyes emotionless, his jaw set grimly. He'd grown into a man. A powerful, terrifying man, but...

"Why did you bring me here?"

Ronin stood suddenly. "Pass."

"Pass?"

"On your questions." Changing the subject, he asked, "Your father is there? I remember him. Talon Lawson. Cassius is holding him?"

"Yes. I was headed to try and see him last night when I saw you...fighting..."

"That shifter is dead. I killed him." He arched his eyebrows. "You should know what I'll do for my people. Ask me if I lost any sleep over his death."

She didn't have to. The dead expression in his

eyes told her enough. He walked to the door and then, hand on the knob, he said, "Your father."

Softly and sadly, she explained, "They took him a week ago. Cassius wants my genetics. My ancestor was one of the founders of the Tarian Pride. They're trying to bring back the founders' bloodlines. I was picked up yesterday. The contract is signed, and I have to go. Today is my pairing day. If I don't show up, they'll kill him. But if I play by their rules, they'll let him go."

Ronin slid her a narrow-eyed glance, his lip snarled up. "Fuck their rules."

And then he walked out the door and let it click closed behind him.

The small noise seemed to echo on and on.

She felt like she was in a dream. Slowly, she stood and padded barefoot to a small sink with a mirror over it. It was one of those old-fashioned white porcelain bowls set on a rustic wooden chest. There was a rusted water spout that she had to pump water from, and the mirror was the same she remembered from all those years ago. In fact, nothing in this room had been changed except the bedding, which was a dark brown now instead of navy blue. The sheets had smelled like Ronin, minus all the blood. What had happened to his shoulder? Had he been stabbed? Shot? That wouldn't surprise her. Tarians wouldn't have any problem using weapons. No honor.

She stared at a reflection she didn't recognize. It was shocking. Not just the bruising and the swelling, the cut lip or the pale skin… She was stunned by how hollow and sad her eyes looked. Gritting her teeth against another wave of grief, she pumped the water handle a few times until the bowl was half full, and then she washed her face. She didn't have her suitcase, so no make-up, but whatever. She didn't have to impress anyone. She wouldn't be here long.

Ronin looked really good. There was something about him that drew her and made her feel safe when she had no right at all to feel that way. Her life had been uprooted, she'd been hurt, and her future was bleak. But for the few minutes when she was talking to him, she'd felt like everything was okay. Or maybe he'd just been a beautiful distraction.

She needed to call Cassius before he did something bad to her father. Her cell phone was probably lying in the woods where Ronin had kidnapped her. Kidnapped her? Had she been kidnapped? Well…that was about right.

A soft knock sounded at the door. "Come in," Emerald said, reaching for a forest green washrag on a small stack of them beside the sink. She gently patted her face dry, careful of the bruised side, and turned to find a silver-haired, familiar-looking woman in the doorway. "Rose?" she asked, the woman's name coasting through her mind and landing on her tongue.

The woman's gray eyebrows arched delicately. "That's right. And you're Emerald. I would know those eyes anywhere, but you've changed, child. Well, I suppose I can't call you 'child' anymore." She smiled kindly, but winced. Slowly, she tucked her hair behind her ear and exposed bruises on her cheek and down her neck that disappeared into her shirt.

"Oh, my gosh," Emerald murmured. "What happened?"

"The Old Tarian Pride took me from my home two nights ago." She studied Emerald's face. "I have a feeling I don't have to tell you what happened to me. You probably understand better than anyone. Ronin came for me. We found you in the woods when we were escaping. Do you remember?"

"I remember a little. I remember being scared. Ronin killed a man."

Rose brushed her fingertips on her injured cheek. "He killed the man who did this to me."

Well, that made a big difference. Ronin wasn't just some murderer at random, going after any Old Tarian lion. He'd avenged Rose and the damage done to her.

"Was my dad in the cabin with you? Talon Lawson?"

Rose frowned and sat on the edge of the mattress. "I didn't see any other prisoners. There was only me in the cabin."

Emerald sighed. That worried her. If they treated their prisoners like they had Rose, how was her father faring now? "Do you have a phone I can borrow?"

"To call Cassius?"

"Yes," she whispered. "I need to go back."

"He knows where you are. He sent a messenger this morning with a letter."

"What did the letter say?"

"Give me back what's mine by two pm, or we kill every last one of you by nightfall."

"Geez, that's horrible," Emerald said, taking a seat

next to the woman. "I didn't ever want to be a part of any war. I just wanted to live free with my dad. Rogue. That was our choice, and Cassius took that away from us. I had a pet goldfish named Chester," she said, drawing her knees to her chest, "a favorite Chinese food delivery service, a crappy job but it was steady income, Sunday dinners with dad, and we were figuring out how to live without my mom. I was finally settling into a life I was happy with again."

"You might not see it now, but everything happens for a reason," Rose murmured.

"Yeah," Emerald agreed, not even trying to hide the lie in her voice. There was no point in dwelling. There was work to be done.

"Ronin is in a meeting with the Pride. You can call Cassius when he makes a decision."

"What kind of decision?" Emerald asked.

Rose only gave her a smirk and shrugged her shoulders. "I don't know. I'm not in the meeting. My choice. I didn't want to be around a bunch of squabbling males right now. Here," she said, handing over a neatly folded pile of clothes.

Frowning, Emerald unfolded them and held them up. It was a plain black fitted T-shirt and a pair of dark-wash skinny jeans with holes expertly ripped into the knees and thighs. The size looked about right. "Were you expecting me?" Emerald joked.

"You? Never. I thought you and your family were free and clear of this place. But now I have an excuse to use my too-young wardrobe. At least that's what Grim teases me about."

Emerald studied Rose's clothes. She was wearing a black tank top under a long-sleeved red flannel button up, and leggings tucked into calf-height leather biker boots. Where her sleeves were rolled up, Rose had a tattoo of the Grim Reaper with a lion's face under the Reaper's hood. A tribute to her grandson, the Grim Reaper? Okay, Rose was a badass. She was like the Tarian Pride lionesses Emerald remembered. Once upon a time, they had been mostly dominant, mouthy, ruthless lionesses, instead of the submissive, broken women she'd met yesterday. Things sure were different here now.

"I'll give you some space to get dressed," Rose murmured as she headed to the door. "Emerald?" she asked suddenly.

"Yes?"

Rose gestured to her face. "None of that is your

fault. If you go back, they'll try to get in your head that you deserve to be treated like that. Like you earned those marks. They'll manipulate you because that's the only move weak men have. Don't listen. You're better than what happened to you." Rose lifted her chin. "You're royalty, and they're the nothings. Not the other way around."

Right as she turned to leave, Emerald blurted out, "Why didn't he Change?"

"Who? Ronin?" Rose asked, her hand on the doorknob.

"Yes. Last night. Why did he kill that man with his bare hands? Why didn't they Change into their lions and fight like the old ways?"

Rose gave her a devilish grin. "Because, child. If Ronin Changed, he would've gone after every Tarian Pride member until they were nothing but a pile of bodies. And he wouldn't have gotten me or you out of there. That lion has a chip on his shoulder the size of a canyon, and the Tarians carved it there. I told him to leave you, you know, just to test him. He couldn't."

"What does that mean?"

Rose shrugged again. "I don't know. All I know is what I saw. He couldn't take his eyes off you, and he couldn't move until he hoisted you up in his arms to take you with us. And today? He was needed to put out all the trouble he stirred up by rescuing me alone, but where do you think he was instead?"

Hope blooming in her chest, Emerald guessed, "In here? With me?"

As Rose made her way out the door, her voice echoed behind her. "Everything happens for a reason."

FIVE

Ronin leaned back in his creaking chair and spun the sharp point of his knife blade onto the letter from Cassius, cutting a small hole and etching a notch into the old wooden meeting table as he did. He read the scribbled words again. *Give me what's mine…*

Mine. Ha. Cassius didn't own Emerald. Did he think abducting her father gave him ownership over her? Ronin was going to kill him—

"—when the time is right!" Terrence yelled, dragging Ronin from the fantasy of locking his teeth on Cassius's exposed throat. Terrence had been talking for a while. Long-winded, that gnarly shifter was.

"They have the numbers," Kannon murmured, "so

we have to be careful. I want as few casualties as possible. On both sides."

"Fuck any side but ours," Ronin growled. "Don't go soft on the Old Tarian Pride, Kannon. They won't go soft on you. They'll cut your life off at the knees at the first chance."

The dark-haired shifter sighed. "What you did last night—"

"Was my choice, had little risk, and had the exact outcome I wanted."

"You killed one of them during a treaty time."

"Would you like me to parade Rose in and show you her face again? I don't know how you think this is supposed to work, but men beating on women will bring out the devil in me faster than anything else."

"Yeah, but we knew him," Gray growled.

Ronin slammed his knife blade deep into the table and leaned forward. "Knowing him doesn't make him a good man."

"You can't just kill everyone who pisses you off—"

"What about war is confusing to you?"

Terrence slammed his open palms on the table and stood, glaring at him. Ronin stood slowly, a snarl in his throat. "Stand. The fuck. Down."

Other than Ronin and Terrence's snarls, dead silence filled the meeting room. Three seconds too long is what it took for Terrence to sit down and angle his face to the side. Ronin looked around. "I know you wanted an Alpha you could control on your throne. And you're taking a big risk backing me. I understand. But I don't do well on leashes. I'm still Alpha. I will make decisions you don't like sometimes, and you know what you can do about it? You can fuckin' deal with it. I'm trying to listen, but if you're gonna keep pushing this kumbaya shit on me, this war is not going to go the way you want. You split off from them for a reason. Because every one of you saw the way the Pride was going and you grew a moral compass somewhere along the way. Good on you. But don't turn soft on me as we're gearing up for war with them. Stay savage. Keep that Tarian fire lit inside of you. Keep the fury until this is done. What have they done to your mothers? Your sisters? Your friends? Don't forget what side you chose. You're acting like Rose wasn't worth the risk, and she was. She is. If one of you were taken, where do you think I would be? I'd be on the same damn rescue mission because I agreed to this—to protecting you. All of you."

"There's rumors you're making Rose your Second," Gray murmured.

"And?" Ronin asked, bristling. He hated this boys-are-better-than-girls crap.

"And when we bring a mate here for you, you'll lift her rank above all of us, won't you? Females at the top and fuck all of us who put you on the throne, right?"

"I haven't decided if I'm agreeing to a pairing or not."

"You will," Kannon said, "because you promised you would pick a mate who would give us allies. We need the Fire Pride. Or the Bonebreakers, the Deadlies, the Bloodwars or, fuck, we would take an alliance with the Dunns if it kept us all from annihilating each other. What is the point of all this if both Tarian Prides kill each other off, and no one is left to make any decisions at all, good or bad? You say we're yours to protect?" Kannon said, clenching his fists in front of him. "Then protect us."

Ronin sighed and looked at the door. His escape, the door that led to the hallway. And at the end of that hallway was his bedroom where Emerald was making his covers smell like her. He went there in his mind. Imagined her smiling at him, like she had when she was a little girl and he'd told the cubs to stop bullying her. He imagined how clear her bright green eyes would be if walked into her room right now. He imagined her happy to see him. But then he remembered her swollen face, and the rage that had nearly made him Change last night returned.

I have to go back. Such sadness had tainted her voice when she'd uttered those words. Pretty Emerald. She would be the gem of the Old Tarian Pride, and Ronin would obsess over whether she was okay there.

But he'd made promises, and a good man didn't break those. A good Alpha protected his Pride, and damn it all, Ronin was determined to be a good Alpha and rehabilitate them. There was this instinct inside him that ordered him to do this. Fixing the Tarians was his purpose.

He locked his arms on the table and sighed. "Bring me files on three females who applied for the match pool. I'll think about it."

"All right. Good," Terrence said, flashing a smile.

"Do you have a preference on hair color?" Or like...bra size?"

Ronin leveled him with a glare. "No. This isn't a love match. It's business. Best allies. That's what you wanted, right?" He couldn't help the disgust in his voice as he made his way to the door.

"Any idea on who will be your Second?" Kannon asked.

Ronin shrugged. "I want Grim."

"The Reaper said no," Gray murmured.

"Then start stepping up," Ronin demanded, walking backward. "This ain't a popularity contest, boys. We ain't votin'. Biggest and baddest wins. And if that's Rose?" He angled his head. "Then she's gonna take Second away from one of you."

Gray pointed at Kannon. "Challenge."

"Aw, fuck!" Kannon said. Gray's lion had a good twenty pounds of muscle on him. Kannon crossed his arms over his chest and gave a cocky grin. "Accepted."

Ronin chuckled as he left the meeting room.

Let the fights begin. And also, let the distraction begin.

Because he was about to make a very, very

questionable decision.

SIX

"Put a coat on," Ronin said, bursting into the room.

Emerald startled hard from where she sat on the bed. She'd been off in la-la land, thinking about how she was going to handle Cassius when she went back, and hadn't even heard Ronin coming down the hall. That, and he could apparently be scary-quiet when he wanted to be.

He leaned against the door frame and crossed his arms over his chest. He'd put on a black sweater that clung to his broad shoulders and tapered at the waist, and his hair was pushed to one side. Those gosh-darn cheekbones and striking blue eyes. Lord, she bet he got a lot of girls' attention.

He dragged his gaze down her body and back up, scratched the corner of his lip with his thumbnail, and smiled slightly. "Is grabbing your tits always your first fear-reaction?"

With a squeak, Emerald removed her hands from the girls and clasped them in her lap. "No."

"Lie. You did it last night, too, when me and Rose found you."

"No, I didn't." Had she? Emerald frowned.

"You definitely did."

After a heaved sigh, she murmured, "Well, this and a million other reasons are why my milkshake doesn't bring the boys to the yard."

"Your milkshake worked just fine for a pussy named Cassius." His voice had darkened on the name.

"Yeah, well, that's not my milkshake. It's just my bloodline. They're beefing up the Tarian Pride over there. I'm surprised you aren't doing the same here. Numbers are power. Dominant cubs are power."

"You aren't dominant, and you're a Lawson. Dominant cubs aren't guaranteed."

Emerald shrugged her shoulders. "Lucky me, I'm a freak."

Ronin chewed the corner of his lip, staring at her

thoughtfully for a few seconds before he twitched his head toward the hallway. "I want to show you something."

"Ronin, I have to go. My dad—"

"I'll take care of that."

"You don't understand. He's all I have left." Emerald's lip trembled, and she hated it. Hated the weakness. She'd been so emotionally raw for the last week, and she was tired.

Ronin's eyes softened, and he approached slow, sat on the bed next to her. After a second of hesitation, he rested his hand on her thigh and squeezed. "I know about not having anything left. I won't let that happen to you." He pulled out his phone and handed it to her. It was open on a text screen.

R: First off, fuck your letter, you don't own Emerald. If I'm to bring her back, I want proof that her dad is alive. It's not that I don't trust you, but I don't fucking trust you. Now, asshole.

C: I would just let you have the tired-looking whore if I wasn't so possessive. And look at you being protective of her. Makes her more interesting to me. She signed the contract. I want her untouched.

R: Too late. You already hit her. I can't wait to have

my hands around your fuckin' throat.

C: She's my mate, I'll do what I want to her face. I'll be giving her a cum facial tonight, Ronin. It's our pairing day. And you'll be sitting up in your little camp thinking about what I'm doing to her. I promise, I won't be gentle.

R: Proof, Cassiass.

C: It's Cassius.

R: (middle finger emoji)

Emerald scrolled to a dim video of her dad. He seemed okay, sitting in a small one-room cabin. A voice off-camera demanded, "Talk."

Emerald clutched the phone with shaking hands as she watched Dad sigh. He was sitting in a chair, elbows on his knees, hands clenched in front of him, eyes glowing gold. Dad wasn't submissive. His lion was a killer, too. He just kept tight control. There was a cut on the side of his head, and streams of dried blood ran down to his unshaven jawline. He looked tired but strong as he leaned back in his chair. He smiled at whoever was behind the camera. "What do you want to talk about pussycat? The claw marks on your face? Looks painful."

A long, low hiss sounded, and Dad gave a feral

chuckle.

Beside her, Ronin snorted. "Respect."

Suddenly Dad looked at the camera and growled, "Cubby, I'm fine." His Adam's apple dipped into his thickly whiskered throat, and he repeated, "I'm fine."

Chills rippled up her arms as the camera went dark.

"See?" Ronin murmured. "He's fine."

"No, you don't get it. That's not what he said."

Ronin squeezed his hand on her thigh again. "What do you mean?"

"That's our code. Cubby is what my mom always called me. 'I'm fine' is our code for 'run and hide.'" Emerald's heart physically hurt. Dad didn't want her to come for him. How could he want her to just leave him there? She wouldn't. Couldn't.

Vision blurring, she read Cassius's message after the video.

C: I want my bitch back right now.

R: She's resting. Noon works better for me.

C: I want you to be the one to bring her to me. I want to see your face when I take her.

"He's playing too nice," she whispered. "He's

going to try and kill you."

Emerald looked up at him, but Ronin didn't look surprised. "I know."

"You can't be the one to take me back. I know his type. You took his toy, and he'll never forgive you. He'll punish you and everyone you care about."

"I took his toy and his prisoner, *and* I killed his Second last night."

"That was his Second?" she asked, voice wrenching up an octave.

Ronin nodded once. "You fell right in the middle of chaos, Em."

Okay, this was all bad news, but he'd called her Em. An accidental smile took her lips. She couldn't help it. She liked the name Em. A nickname from a nice man. A nice, murdery man.

"I remember the night the council told the Pride they'd killed you," she said. "It was a few nights after the Reaper had been born. Leon called a meeting, and his hands were covered in blood. He said the culling had begun with you. They would get rid of the lions who didn't match their plans for the future of the Pride. He talked for a long time, but I didn't hear his words after that. I sat on this old splintered bench between my mom and dad, staring at Leon's bloody hands. They were still wet. He talked with his hands a lot, and I couldn't take my eyes off them. It was the first time I'd ever felt empty. I watched you when I was a cub after you protected me. To me, you were my friend, and when I saw your blood on Leon's hands...it felt like someone took a piece of my heart and I never got it back."

"I watched you, too, you know. Way before I beat that kid up. I remember you always looked down at your shoes. You had these little pink converses. I used to wait for you to look up because your eyes were pretty. That was the game. Seeing if I could get you to look up but not get busted. I would toss pebbles near you or make noises. Try to get your attention without you knowing I was trying to get your attention. Because I liked when you looked up. When you looked around at the world." Ronin angled his head back and pulled the edge of his beard out of the way. There was a long red scar there. "Leon tried to slit my throat. I fought like hell, and he didn't get the job done before Damon showed up. Beaston was stitching me up on our way to the Furers. I thought I would surely die before we got where we were going, but he told me he was a Gray Back, and Gray Backs could stitch up anything." She reached up and drew her finger down the scar, but Ronin grabbed her hand and his eyes flashed with anger. "Don't you ever let a man hit you again, Em. You hear me? You're a fuckin' lioness. A Tarian lioness. I don't care if you're submissive. If a man hurts you?" His face twisted with fury. "You hurt them back."

Before she could change her mind, Emerald slid her arms around his waist and squeezed. Ronin froze, and every muscle went tense under her embrace. She could've been hugging a boulder. She didn't care, though. What did she have to lose? She had three hours before she returned to Hell. "Thank you for that day on the playground. I always remembered you. Even when I thought you were dead, you were remembered. I used memories of you to remind myself there were good people in the world."

Ronin softened and slipped his hands gently around her, pulling her against him like she was fragile. "Oh, Em. You've been mistaken. I'm not good. But I will make sure you're okay."

"It won't be okay if you're the one to take me back to Cassius. I want to go alone."

"Not a chance in he—"

"This is my choice. I choose to go back."

"You choose him?"

Heart banging against her sternum, she croaked out, "Yes."

"Lie. There was no truth in that answer at all. I'm going to ask you that again before today is done, and next time I want the truth."

"I thought you died once," she whispered. "It was awful, and I mourned a boy I barely knew. And now I care more. You've showed me kindness twice now. On the playground and last night. And for some reason, it means a lot. I really feel it. I want you to live."

"Sweet Kitty," Ronin said low. "I'm not the boy I once was." And that wasn't a lie. His voice was scary-steady when he uttered that promise. "You want to go back, I'll take you back." His face changed suddenly, and a snarl ripped out of him, his entire body clenching as he tore his gaze away from hers and stared at the wall across the room. He was hugging her so tight, her back popped a few times. Felt kinda good, but he murmured "sorry" in a low and gritty voice. "We have three hours until we need to head that way. Let's take a break."

"A break from what?"

He dragged fiery green-gold eyes with small pupils back to her. *Hello, lion.* "A break from both of our lives." When his gaze dipped to her lips, she thought he would kiss her.

Do it.

He smelled so good, and his power had enveloped them in a little bubble of safety. All of her chaotic emotions overwhelmed her and made her desperate to get lost in his strength for a second. To not feel like crying, worrying, or mourning for a moment. To not think at all. And Ronin could give that to her with a kiss, consequences be damned.

Be bold.

Three hours, and she would disappear again. She would be a ghost, living from one second to the next with no purpose. But here and now, she could be alive. She counted to three as she searched his face and then brushed her fingertips down his beard. He rolled his eyes closed and huffed a breath, then opened his eyes to watch her again.

Take a chance.

Because when else would she have this

opportunity? Emerald stretched her neck up slightly, but just when she was inches from his lips, he touched the injured side of her face gently and shook his head.

His eyes swam with some dark emotion she didn't understand. "You don't belong to me. Not like this." And then he dropped his head and clamped his teeth gently on her neck. She froze there under the intimate touch, shocked, turned on…devoted to this moment with him. It was the only bite she would ever really want, and for the rest of her life, she would hold this memory. The one where she wished for a life that wasn't in her stars.

Ronin released her skin, released her from his arms, released her completely. Just…let her go. He stood and left the room. "I'll meet you outside."

And for the second time today, the closing of the door felt symbolic, not just physical.

Emerald had never been more confused by a man in her entire life.

He was a study of opposites.

Moral compass but a killer.

Kidnapper but counting down the hours until he took her back.

Affectionate but left as soon as she got close.

I'm not the boy I once was.

No, he was not. And what was she? The exact same. Submissive, helpless to a bully on the playground and in need of a hero. But now it was on a bigger scale. Helpless to Cassius's bullying, she needed Ronin to save her.

What would she learn about herself, good and bad, if she was put in a position where she had to stand alone?

The grit in her wanted to know. She didn't know how she was going to do it, but she was going to escape Ronin to keep him safe, and she was going to face Cassius on her own.

And fuck that contract.

She didn't have a plan, but she was going to figure out a way to get her dad out of there. To get them both out of there.

No man would ever hurt her again. No man had that right. In shock, she had taken it from Cassius, and the shame still heated her cheeks. But Ronin had gritted out a reminder. She *was* a Tarian lioness, and he was right. It didn't matter if she was submissive; she was still valuable. She was still a person. She'd hated the Tarians for so long, but those words had filled her with the ghost of a feeling she'd never thought she would associate with her history—pride. She remembered those Tarian lionesses of her childhood. Warriors. Hunters. So the Old Tarian Pride had been replacing those badasses with the easily breakable. Fuck the males for *their* weakness. She remembered what she could be.

The image of the hate twisting Ronin's face flashed through her mind. *You hurt them back.*

A big piece of her wanted him to be proud of her.

Deep inside of her, the lioness perked up her ears and paid attention.

"Did you hear that?" Emerald asked her lion softly. "He called you Sweet Kitty. Stop being sweet. You have teeth."

SEVEN

Ronin shouldn't be doing this. He shouldn't be spending extra time with Emerald. He should be distancing himself and handling the million chores he had on his plate today.

But if he *was* going to do this, if he was going to go after Cassius one-on-one, he needed to let himself feel for Emerald. He needed her to fuel his fury.

Fuck taking her back. Cassius had plans. Probably ambush. He would probably have his Pride attack before Ronin and Emerald even reached their territory. That's what Alphas with no honor did. Ronin was okay with it because he was ready. Mentally, he was prepared. The war had been dragging too long, both sides putting off annihilation, but he wasn't here to tiptoe around this. He was here to change the ending of the Tarian story. It's why he'd agreed to come back in the first place.

The day the council had been killed, Zeke, Alpha of the tiger shifter clan called the Furers, and Ronin's adoptive father, had pulled him into a Crew meeting.

"It's time," he'd said. "You've been trained. You're ready to take a Pride. Go take back the one that tried to end you. I see it in you, that anger. It'll never go away until you get your revenge. You want revenge? Go poison that Pride from the inside out with our ways. Poison them with honor."

The Challenge Gray had given Kannon was in full swing. Their lions were Changed and brawling in the middle of a loose circle with the Pride looking on and cheering for favorites. It was loud, but that was just fine with Ronin.

Ronin knelt in the snow and blew out a long, frozen breath, rubbed his cold hands together. His lion always felt better outside, but he still hadn't adjusted to the cold again. The Furers were down in Louisiana where it stayed relatively warm. He'd forgotten just how frigid winters could be in Colorado.

It was taking Emerald a long time to put a jacket on. Perhaps she'd decided not to come out here. Maybe he'd scared her with that little bite on her neck. Hell, he understood. He'd scared himself with it. He'd tried to back away from the kiss, but his lion had taken over and laid his teeth possessively on her neck, teasing her with a claiming mark.

He was losing his damn mind around her.

Maybe he really did need to find a mate.

Maybe not one like Emerald, who would be broken by what was happening between the Tarian Prides.

A snarl rattled up his throat. *She isn't fragile. Shut up, Lion.*

Ronin swallowed the sound down, eyes on the front door. The bruises on her face that wouldn't heal fast enough and the easy tears in her eyes said differently. She might not be fragile, but she hadn't realized her strength yet. And he would be damned if he was so selfish that he would ask her to find that strength by putting her through war.

He just needed to get her out of here. No...it was more than that. Ronin frowned. He needed to keep her safe.

The front door creaked open, and Emerald stepped out onto the front porch. She didn't see him right away, so he stilled. He liked watching her when she didn't know. He'd done it as a cub, and had done it again last night while she was sleeping. What a fucking creeper he'd turned out to be.

She frowned in the direction of the fight, but when a squirrel rustled a tree branch, Emerald's attention darted to it. He could see her profile from here. High cheek bones and dark eyebrows. Raven-colored hair that tumbled down her shoulders like black waves. She'd washed all of her make-up away, but she was still a stunner. She wasn't one of those skinny girls the Pride was probably looking to put on the throne beside him. Nah, that wasn't his type. His type was Emerald. She had full, soft-lookin' tits and an ass he could grab when he was fucking her. Just the mental image of him railing her on her back, her spine arched under him, his name on her lips, how tight and wet she would feel, made his dick hard and too thick to kneel in this position comfortably. When he stood slowly, she arched her gaze to him. Her full lips turned up in a sweet smile. Had anyone smiled like that before when they'd seen him? He couldn't remember a single time.

"Hi," he murmured.

She inhaled deeply and then grinned even bigger as she said, "Hi, yourself."

Something was different about her, but he couldn't put his finger on it. He held up a giant paper grocery bag, the meal he'd thrown together for them. "Do you want to do a hike and have lunch with me?"

Her cheeks turned a pretty shade of pink as she nodded. God, those gorgeous green eyes. It was hard to look away from them. As she approached, her thick-soled boots made crunching sounds through the snow.

He said, "You don't look down as much anymore."

"Well, not here. No one's putting me in my place here." Her jacket was open, so Ronin set the bag of food down in the snow and pulled her closer by the open flaps of her coat. As he zipped her up, he said, "No one will put you in your place here."

"Why not?" she asked cheekily.

Pretty girl. He didn't like hurting girls, but she should keep her distance today. He would have to walk a fine line between letting his lion get protective but not bonding them. He didn't want to make it harder for her to leave.

Keep her safe. And he would, even if it meant from himself.

He gestured to the fight as they swung a wide berth around it. "You wouldn't even guess how many of those fights I've been in. My destiny is a bloody one, Em. You should know that before I tell you things that will take the smile from your face."

"What do you mean?" she asked, her attention on the two bloody lions that were locked up in battle.

Terrence was on the outskirts, not paying attention to the fight. Instead, he was tracking Ronin and Emerald with narrowed, suspicious eyes. He was going to have to bring Terrence back in line sooner rather than later. That lion had been pushing Ronin lately. But it would have to wait until tomorrow, if he survived. Right now, he had three precious hours with Em. Ripping his gaze away from Terrence, he said, "I mean, I don't necessarily want to hurt you. We just aren't on the same path of destruction. I want to keep it that way." He zipped her jacket up to her neck and took a step away, picked up the sack, and started walking toward the woods. "No one will put you in your place because you don't belong here."

He heard it—a little whoosh of breath like she'd been hurt by his words. Too fragile, and it made him feel things. Soft things that were bad for an Alpha on a mission. He needed to keep his focus.

Behind him, Emerald cleared her throat. "You have a lot of tattoos."

An out—that was what she offered him. An out from the painful, awkward moment that hung in the air between them. Right at the edge of the trees, he stopped and waited for her to catch up. "I got my first one the year after I joined the Furers."

"The tiger Crew?"

He nodded. "I was a hell-raiser there. Mad at the world, missing Grim—"

"I remember you two were really close," she said, picking her way carefully through the brush beside him. The trail here was years overgrown and barely visible anymore.

"Yeah. He was a brother to me. I spent so much time with him and Rose, they were like a family to me when I lived here. And then suddenly being ripped away and placed in a Crew of strangers? They took me in, but Tigers stick with tigers. It wasn't their idea to bring in a lion cub with the Tarian Pride's death-mark on his neck. I think Damon bribed them. Or threatened them."

Ronin chuckled at the memory of the entire Crew going quiet every time someone mentioned the Blue Dragon. "And I wasn't super-enjoyable to be around. I fought everyone all the time, for any reason at all. I was just pissed down to my soul. I got passed around from family to family, until finally the Alpha, Zeke, came to visit me. He was a bachelor tiger, a total monster, got to be Alpha by brawling his way to the top and stepping on every bit of political tradition in the process. Old, scarred-up, gnarly beast of a man. I remember he found me sitting on a woodpile, not doing the chores my foster family at the time had asked me to do, and he was this tall, barrel-chested man. I was thin as a whip at the time, hadn't started getting my size on me yet. He had this great big old beard and dominance out the ass, and it was hard to even breathe around him." Ronin moved a branch aside for Emerald to pass. "He asked me, 'Boy, do you even know what you're fighting for?' And I couldn't answer intelligently at the time because I didn't know why I was so angry, so I said, 'Hey, Zeke, why don't you fuck off,' and before the last word was out of my mouth, he had my shirt in his fist and had dragged me within an inch of his face. I could feel his snarl, he was that close."

"Oh, my gosh," Em murmured. "What happened then?"

"Well, I about pissed myself because I thought it was finally happening, I was gonna die, but he pulled his lips back over some razor-sharp teeth and said, 'You're my cub now.'" Ronin couldn't help his smile. "You know how degrading it is to hear you're some stranger's cub at age seventeen? I thought I was grown! I thought I didn't need anyone in the world, and then Zeke comes in and basically says, 'Look, baby, you're mine to bottle feed now until you learn to handle your shit.' I think my pride circled the toilet that day. And it's not like I could say, 'Polite decline,' to the Alpha. He was Zeke. He was fuckin' terrifying, twice my size, and dominant as hell. I was shaking in my boots while trying to act tough."

"What did you say?"

There was a smile in her voice, so Ronin looked over at her to see the curve to her lips. So pretty.

"Well, what else could I say? I looked him square in the eyes and said..." He drew it out as he helped her over a fallen log in the trail. "Yes, sir."

Em snorted and then laughed so loud it echoed through the wild Tarian woods. "You weren't so tough back then."

"Oh, fuck no. I *thought* I was tough as old leather that first year, but it took one close encounter with Zeke, and I was docile as a kitten. He told me from then on, I wouldn't be fighting his Crew. No more challenging the shifter kids at school or fighting the less dominant adults. He said if I had an itch to fight, he was going to teach me how to really fight."

"How?"

"By fighting him."

"While he was Changed?" Em asked, her voice jacked up an octave.

"Yep. And you should see his tiger. He's a monster through and through. He's still Alpha of the Furers. Longest lasting Alpha in Tiger Crew history."

"Wow," Em said on a frozen breath. "And he was the one who took you in."

"Yeah. I know I didn't find my place until I was seventeen, but it feels like between Rose and him, I had it all right. Maybe not a lot of people would think that way, but for me...well...I'm grateful for what I had."

"Was he good to you?"

"Very. Very hard on me, but very good. He didn't do anything that wasn't teaching me a lesson. He turned me into a man."

"I would like to meet him someday," she said softly, her eyes on the ground again as she walked.

Staring at her profile, trying to read her expression, that's when it hit him. It had been bothering him that he couldn't figure out what was different about her. Ronin pulled her to an abrupt stop and hooked a finger under her chin, lifted her face. The bruising had faded, barely even there, the swelling gone, and the split in her lip was just an angry red line that would be nothing more than a faint scar in a day or two.

"Your healing."

"What about it?" she asked, gripping his wrist.

"It sped up."

"Oh." Em brushed her fingers over her cheek. "My lioness came back."

See? Not fragile, his inner lion rumbled.

Huh.

"My mom passed away a few years ago," she said

suddenly. "And it's just been me and my dad ever since. I don't feel sorry for myself and I don't want pity that she's gone. I talked about it with Dad so much. I feel lucky I got that much time and the relationship I had with her. She was really good to me. My best friend. And I just hope to be half the woman she is someday."

"I remember your mom," Ronin said thoughtfully. "I've been remembering a lot since I moved back here. She was a badass like your dad. One of those intimidating Tarian lionesses you didn't fuck with. And I remember how the council treated her and your dad when they found out you were born a submissive. They stripped your family of their rank in the Pride, dropped them to the very bottom. Good on your parents for leaving. They deserved a better life."

"We left the night after Leon had your blood on his hands. We left with almost nothing and rebuilt our lives completely. It was scary but worth it."

"Did you have boyfriends?" he asked carefully. "Not that I care...just...making conversation."

She was slightly ahead of him now and tossed him a mischievous grin over her shoulder like she'd heard the lie in his voice. He was glad he had a beard.

Beards hid blushes.

"I had a few. All humans."

"Whoa, scandalous," he teased.

"I wish. I am a boring good girl and zero percent scandalous. I think my life would be different if I had rebelled. Human boys didn't care about me being submissive. Shifters...well, they have more of a problem with it."

"What do you mean?"

I tried to date a bear shifter when I was a few years out of high school. At first, when we were getting to know each other, it was easy and fun, but he would get domineering. I don't even think that was his natural habit. I think that was just his bear's reaction to my lioness. She's..."

"She's what?"

Em inhaled deeply and heaved a sigh. "She makes me invisible."

Why did his chest hurt at her admission? "You're wrong, Em. You couldn't be invisible if you tried."

"That used to be my biggest fear," she said, picking her way through a narrow passage of brush.

"What?"

"Being invisible."

"Mmm." Every instinct in him wanted to trail his fingers down to the small of her back as she moved with him, just to touch her. But he didn't. She deserved better than any future he could offer her. "And what's your biggest fear now?"

She turned to him and gave him a sad smile. "Not being invisible enough."

Fuck, she was talking about Cassius. About his attention on her, about him hunting her.

She perked up and forced a smile. "I've just figured out where you're taking me."

"You recognize it?"

She looked around the woods. "At first, I didn't. This trail is really old. Probably no one has been out here in years." Her dark eyebrows lowered over those striking green eyes. "Have you been out here since you moved back?"

Ronin shook his head. "I didn't even think about this place until I realized who you were. Now it seems fitting. We'll see it for the first time together."

Lifting her chin, Em twirled her wrist regally and then offered her hand, palm up. "Shall we, then?"

He shouldn't touch her. If he did, he would want more. That's what had happened when he'd hugged her earlier, but Emerald was an addiction he didn't understand. She quieted the anger inside of him, and it felt good to think of something other than war. It felt good to think of love instead. Love? God, he needed to get ahold of himself. And he would. After one more touch. After he touched her, then he would probably get ahold of himself again.

Ronin slid his hand against hers, squeezed it, and dropped them to their sides, and then he led her through the last of the trees into the clearing. And as they came to a stop in the untouched snow, he didn't let her hand go. He didn't want to. It was warm and soft and little against his large one, and he wanted to take care of something fragile right now.

She isn't fragile.

Her chest was heaving as she scanned the old dilapidated playground. The swing set was still standing, and the merry-go-round was still functioning. It spun slowly in the wind with the softest sound of metal on metal. The slide had long ago toppled to its side, and the wood of the playset had rotted to splinters. The old benches where the moms used to chat while their cubs played weren't there anymore, and the old splashpad they played on in the summers was buried under piles of snow.

"You know, I have all these bad memories of living here," Em said softly. "They overshadowed the good ones. Do you remember how many cubs the Pride used to have?"

"A lot. We had some fun days out here," Ronin murmured low as a myriad of memories of play-dates drifted across his mind. Emerald was there for several of them.

"The Pride was awful to outsiders and submissives, but it had good parts, too," she said forgivingly.

"I have an admission, one I've never told anyone." He could see her look up at him out of his peripheral, but he couldn't look in her eyes when he said this. He would chicken out. "Those few good parts of the Pride? I want those to outnumber the bad someday. And I want to be the one to make it happen."

"Even if it means killing off the Old Tarian Pride completely?"

Ronin nodded. "Even so. I would carry all of that blood on my soul if I could fix us."

"When I saw you beating that lion last night, I thought you were a killer."

"I am."

"No. You are just a man who sticks up for what is right, no matter the cost, no matter the consequences, no matter what. Killers take life for fun."

Ronin let her see the devil in his smile as he promised, "Cassius will be fun."

Em's eyes went shocked and round. "What?"

Ronin strode toward the merry-go-round, bag of food swinging in his hand. "Stop thinking nice things about me, Em. Your faith in me won't change what I am."

EIGHT

"My butt is frozen," Emerald said with a laugh. The cold metal of the merry-go-round was no joke. Her cheeks were numb.

Ronin laughed and shrugged out of his jacket from where he sat across from her.

"Wait, what are you doing?"

"I should've brought a blanket. I thought the benches would still be here."

"You'll freeze without your coat."

Ronin made a soft click behind his teeth and told her to, "Lift up."

Shocked at his sweet manners, she lifted off the gently spinning merry-go-round and let him tuck his jacket under her. "That..." She cleared her throat. "But you're a Tarian lion."

Ronin snorted. "I don't think you mean that as a compliment. You could just say 'thank you.'"

She belted out a laugh and nodded, her cheeks heating with embarrassment. "Thank you."

Finished tucking his coat under her, he locked his arms on either side of her hips and grinned. "I only brought enough food for me, so there you go. There's the rude-ass Tarian in me."

Scoffing, she dropped her mouth open. "I knew it."

Ronin snorted and started to ease away, but Emerald cupped his cheeks fast. His beard was so soft she couldn't help wanting to touch it. To touch him. He froze, and the laughter left his eyes.

"I'm sorry," she whispered.

Ronin searched her face as he murmured, "Lie."

"Yeah, that was a lie. I like to pet you." Emerald grinned big, and the chuckle that Ronin gave warmed her soul.

He pushed forward and rubbed his cheek against hers, and God, it felt so good to be greeted like that. It was a lion's way of showing affection, and he was doing it as a man. Easing back, he rubbed his face against the other side, the side Cassius had hit, and she uttered a helpless sound.

"Did I hurt you?" he rumbled.

"No, it feels so good." Could he hear her pounding heartbeat? "I wish we lived in a different world."

Ronin sat back on his bent knees, resting his strong hands on her thighs. "What do you mean?"

"Today is my pairing day." She couldn't meet his gaze even if she tried. "And it's all wrong."

Ronin lifted her chin. "You're breaking the rules. No thinking about what will happen. You're safe."

For now. It would probably be better if she'd never felt this at all—this connection with Ronin. It was addictive.

"Then can I tell you whatever I want? For the next..." She checked her phone screen. It was full of messages from Derek cussing her out. She did her best to ignore that part and look at the time. "Two hours and fifteen minutes?"

Ronin sighed and rested the top of his head against her neck, forcing her to look up at the gray storm clouds above. Affectionate man. He was even better than she remembered. His touch made her steady.

"For the next two hours and fifteen minutes, you can tell me anything. And then we have work to do."

She didn't understand that last part. Running her hands through his hair, scratching his scalp slightly with her nails, she said, "I know we barely know each other. I have what I learned about you as a cub and what I've learned about you in the last day, but that's all. But inside, I feel happy when you touch me, look at me, or when I think of you. And I'm going to hold onto these three hours for always, just so you know. It'll be a good memory, like when you protected me here on this playground. If this was a different world, I would let myself have a crush on you, and want you to take me to a movie. And kiss me. And sleep beside me. And for us to learn every single thing about each other, good and bad."

A growl rattled his throat and Ronin backed away. "Rules, Em."

"You won't hurt me if I break them." Not like Cassius.

The woods spun slowly around them. The merry-go-round was easy at turning, and the wind kept them moving. He stared off into the world, turning around them, while they sat still. "The Pride is finding me a mate."

Oh, what those words did to her heart. They physically hurt. "Why?"

"Because we need allies. And a pairing secures them."

She blinked hard and stared at the paper bag of food. "Okay."

She gritted her teeth against jealousy because she had no right to it. Instead, she forced a smile and began to remove the wrapped sandwiches from the bag.

"Just okay?" he asked.

"It's fine. I have no right to have any feelings about who you pair up with." A wave of bitter envy washed through her, and a snarl rattled her throat. Emerald gasped and clamped her hands over her mouth. "I'm sorry. My lioness doesn't to that."

"She doesn't growl?"

"No. Never. Not even when I Change. She just crawls around on her belly and cowers a lot. She doesn't even hiss!"

Another growl tickled her chest. Oh, dear goodness, this was mortifying. She rambled, "The one time I need to be an emotionless girl, and the animal does this."

"An emotionless girl? That's not you."

"Yes it is!" Okay, she was panicking. "I think you should take your jacket back."

Ronin canted his head and narrowed his eyes, and why was he smiling? "You like me."

"No. No, no, no, you are just a boy. From my childhood. Whom I can't have a crush on." *Walls up, woman!* "Who I thought kindly of, but I'm promised to someone else—"

"Who's an abusive asshole."

"And you're promised to someone else—"

"Not yet. Not technically. The Pride is just looking at applications."

Emerald's mouth flopped open and she scoffed. "Oh, you're going to let them choose who you end up with for the rest of your life? That's great. I hope she's super duper nice—"

"Yeah, that's what I told them. Except without the 'super duper' added in there," he murmured, his eyes narrowing with suspicion. Oh yeah, he was definitely starting to figure out she was turning into a lunatic!

"Don't invite me to your wedding," she demanded sarcastically.

"Oh...my...God."

"Why are you smiling like that?" she shrieked like a psychopath.

"Because this is fuckin' awesome. Keep going. Jealousy looks hot on you."

She meant to flip him off, but her hands got stuck in her jacket pockets. "I don't need this—this—"

"Insanity?"

"Stop. Smiling!" she yelped, struggling to exit the merry-go-round. She fell. Yep. She totally busted it, slipped on the metal edge, and went down hard in the snow. And how did she react? She didn't. She laid there in the snow looking up at the sky like a frozen starfish.

Ronin's stupid, sexy, grinning face appeared over her. "Sooo...do you want to bone now, or...?"

"This isn't funny," she muttered, covering her burning cheeks. "You turned me into a crazy person."

"Good dick'll do that."

"Ronin," she snarled.

"It's good. Trust me."

Emerald bit her bottom lip hard to hide her smile because this man did not need encouragement. She grabbed a handful of snow beside her and blasted it up into his face. He was laughing as he shook the frozen stuff out of his hair. Laughing!

"Oh, yeah, this is hilarious. You're gonna pair up with someone you've never met and I'm marrying the dude who split my lip first meeting, so laugh it up, Chuckles! Our lives are *so* entertaining."

"I mean…it's a little funny, Sweet Kitty."

"Don't call me that. I'm changing. I'm mean and terrifying now. I growled. Listen! I'm still growling."

He hopped off the merry-go-round and landed right beside her in the snow. "All I hear is purring."

"It's not a purr. You make me furious. I'm growling."

His eyes sparked goldish-green. "I could make you purr."

"Eeep!" Emerald covered her face with her hands to hide from him. "Dirty."

"Not me. I'm a gentleman."

"I'm pretty sure gentlemen don't bite a girl's neck the first time they meet them."

Ronin tugged her hand away from her face and pulled her to her feet so fast her stomach dipped like she was on a roller coaster. Whoa.

"Make a fist."

"What?"

"Come on." Ronin held his clenched hands up to his face and said it again. "Make a fist."

"I'm not going to fight you."

"You will fight someone at some point, Em. I want you to know how to throw a punch."

"But...I'm not a fighter."

He raised his eyebrows in warning and shook his head. "Wrong attitude."

Emerald clenched her hands at her sides. She did this. She got embarrassed around men like Ronin. Strong, to-the-point, dominant, confident men. Sometimes they swallowed up everything that made Emerald...Emerald.

"You're blushing. Why? Anger?" he asked.

"No." She clenched her teeth and held up her fists. "I get shy. And I don't like making mistakes."

"Tuck your thumb, and hold that hand a little closer to your face. Cassius is right-handed. Protect that left side a little more."

"How do you know he's right-handed?" she asked making the adjustments.

He reached forward and tucked her thumbs around her fists better. "The left side of your face looked like hamburger until an hour ago. That's his dominant hand."

"Oh." Emerald frowned. "I should've known that."

Ronin threw a fake jab. "Good. You dodged it."

"It's not very gentlemanly to throw punches at a girl who just got hurt less than a day ago."

"This life moves on, Em. Learn that fast. What happened yesterday is the past. Learn from it but don't let it stunt you." When he took another jab, she blocked him. "Good. Now punch my hands. Put force behind each hit. I want you confident before you see any of the Old Tarian Pride again."

She swung, and her knuckles made contact with his open palm. The sound of it reminded her of last night when Ronin had been beating that man who'd hurt Rose. "You don't like when men hurt women, do you?" she asked, hitting him again.

"No. It feeds a fire in me." He showed her how to put her weight behind a swing and told her, "Harder."

She pelted him for a few minutes, careful to mind his instructions because he was giving her a gift. If he couldn't be around to make her safe, he was giving her a little weapon. A way to defend herself when her lioness wouldn't. Good man.

He spun her and wrapped his hand around her throat. "If anyone grabs you from behind," he rattled into her ear, "you throw an elbow straight back." He drew her arm straight back, showing her. "If your lioness won't help you in a fight, don't Change, find a weapon, fight dirty. I don't give a fuck about honor if you're being attacked." He spun her back and gripped the back of her hair, easing her face back gently. "Protect your throat at all costs."

Those words echoed over and over in her head. Protect your throat at all costs. She wasn't invisible to Ronin. He cared. Even when she wasn't around, she had a feeling he would still care.

She lifted up on her toes suddenly and pressed her lips against his. It happened fast. Just a little smack, and she lowered back down, just as shocked as Ronin looked.

"Why did you do that?" Ronin looked so stunned. Powerful legs splayed, eyes fierce, hair mussed, a foreground for the snowy winter woods. He took up so much more space than a man should. He was everywhere.

"I...I'm sorry."

He shook his head slowly. "Don't ever apologize

unless you do something wrong."

"But I thought—"

Ronin closed the two feet of space between them and gripped the back of her neck as his lips crashed onto hers. She should've felt trapped, but she didn't. Instead, she felt enveloped, warm, and steady. The slight pressure of his mouth on hers erased the rest of the world. In this moment, only she and Ronin existed. There was no fear, no problems to solve, nothing. There was just the taste and the feel of his body. Getting lost in him, she slid her hands up his stomach, over the mounds of his abs, to his stone-hard chest. Every part of his body was tense except for his lips. Those moved against hers smoothly. Up, up she slid her hands, memorizing his body through the material of his sweater. Ronin grabbed her hand suddenly and dragged it to the hem of his pants, under his shirt, and then pressed her palm against his stomach. He moaned against her lips as she drew a small circle with her thumb on his warm skin, right over his belt buckle.

As she ghosted her fingertips right along the edge of his underwear, Ronin dragged her closer. She parted her lips for him. God, it had been so long since she'd kissed anyone. But this wasn't nerve-racking. It wasn't something she'd had time to overthink, and he was in such control, she was just along for the ride. He slanted his head to the other side and pressed his tongue into her mouth. Oh, the taste of him. Her head was swimming with happiness. She'd never been more turned on so quickly. Carefully, she pushed her fingertips into his jeans and felt the head of his swollen cock. There was a bead of moisture at the tip, and she felt like she was losing her mind with lust. Maybe her lioness was going into heat or something. Or maybe Ronin was just that sexy. So enthralling and all-encompassing that her body couldn't resist him.

His fingers dug into her hip, and his thumb stroked her cheek as he kissed her. When she brushed the head of his dick again, he groaned and rocked his hips toward her. Ronin scooped her up suddenly and sat on the merry-go-round, settling her on his lap. He cupped her cheeks and slowed the kiss. His tongue went shallow into her mouth as if he was tasting her. His affections turned to fingertips in her hair and then knuckles dragging down the arm of her jacket. His lips stayed on her, breaking only to change angles. She got to know the exact way he liked to make-out because he took his time. He didn't rush, didn't push, but slowed them down instead. He dropped them right in the moment and allowed them to stay there instead of seeing how far they could go.

Emerald was falling so hard for this man. For his heart, his mind, and his body as well.

It shouldn't happen like this—falling. She should've toed the cliff for a while and watched to find the safest place to jump. She should've observed and found the deepest waters below. She should've done this safely.

But she didn't.

Instead, she'd come barreling for the cliff and leapt, not checking if there were rocks below or waves. Not checking how far or short the drop was.

Was this how it was supposed to happen?

A heart recognizing a heart as its own?

A body recognizing a body as its own?

It was terrifying and exciting all at once.

Afraid he was cold because he was currently sitting on top of his jacket, she unzipped hers and wrapped the sides around him as best as she could, smashing her chest onto his.

Ronin smiled against her lips and grabbed her ass

under her jacket. His kisses became little sexy smacks until he finally rested his forehead against hers and sighed. "We need to go back to the house."

"Noooooo," she murmured. "Five more minutes."

Ronin laughed and hugged her tight. "As much as I would love to spend the next seven to ten days here with you, I have a meeting to call." He looked up at the sky. "We have about an hour before I need to leave to meet with Cassius."

Oh, she hadn't missed it. He'd said only that *he* needed to leave. Not both of them. Emerald narrowed her eyes at him. "What are you planning?"

"Nothing at all," he said smoothly. Too smoothly.

"Also, did you just look at the sun to gauge the time? Like Crocodile Dundee?"

"I learned a lot in my time with the tigers."

Utterly impressed, she muttered, "That's the sexiest thing ever. Any time in the next hour you want to make out some more, just do that again."

Ronin snorted. "I set my alarm on my phone. It's been vibrating in my pocket for the last ten minutes. I just didn't want to stop kissing you."

"Oh." Emerald giggled. "I'm really gullible around you."

"It's pretty damn cute." His lips were all curved up in a smile as he stared at her with those bright blue eyes. "You're really pretty." He said it fast and then gave this hotboy chuckle at himself and shook his head, cleared his throat. In a softer voice, he told her, "You're hard to look away from, but it's more than you just being beautiful, Em. You're so different from everyone else."

"What do you mean?" she asked softly, touching his beard.

"You're submissive, but strong. Loyal. Brave."

"No one has ever mistaken me for brave before."

"Then no one really knew you. Your dad's in danger so you're doing what it takes to save him. You had two options. Run, like he asked you to, or go right into a terrifying situation that will swallow up your whole life, just to make sure he's safe. I don't care what anyone else would call that. I see it how it is. You're brave, Em. And funny, beautiful, and resilient. And even if your lioness tries to be invisible, I hope someday I get the chance to see her."

And because she had nothing to lose, she asked, "Do you want to see her now?"

It was the biggest risk of all. Letting this dominant

Tarian Alpha see her biggest shame. But why not? He'd passed every test she hadn't even realized she'd been giving him.

Sure, he was dangerous, but deep down to her soul, she knew he was only dangerous to the ones who hurt his people. And just as deep down, where she would never admit it out loud because she knew her reality, she wished she could be one of his people, too.

"You would Change for me?" he asked softly.

"It's the only chance we have," she said, trying so hard to keep the sadness from her voice. That was the rule. Stay in the moment.

Slowly, she dismounted his lap and unzipped her jacket. Heat was already creeping up her neck, and she couldn't meet his gaze. She shrugged out of her jacket and kicked off her snow boots before carefully tucking her socks into them. The snow was freezing against her bare feet.

Okay, now for the big stuff. When she glanced up at Ronin, he was watching her with fiery gold eyes. When she hesitated at the hem of her sweater, he stood and turned around, giving her privacy. She kind of wished she could've made it sexy and stripped down for him without going all shy. Nudity was second nature to most shifters, but not to her.

She folded her clothes and stood there with her bare skin getting whipped by the wind. "I don't Change around people."

"Why not?"

"Because of how my animal is. I was rogue with my parents for so long I didn't really get caught in the situation too often. Not since I was a cub." The last sentence shook because she was shivering, from cold and from nerves. "Okay, here I go."

She inhaled deeply and closed her eyes. Usually, it took a long time because the lion was shy, but today was different. She'd been watching Ronin, fully aware, fully awake, and she was right there under her skin, waiting for permission to take over. The pain was blinding, but it was over so fast, it left her breathless on all fours, stunned that she wasn't writhing on the ground, waiting for every bone to break and every muscle to take on a new shape. It was a second, maybe two, and then she was this. She was the lioness. The Invisible.

Daring a look at Ronin, to Emerald's mortification, he was facing her now. Had he seen the

Change? She didn't know. All she knew was the look on his face made her heart pound harder. She wished she had more control, but this body was the property of the lioness. She crouched slowly to her belly and exposed her neck. Like always.

Ronin knelt beside her and dragged his eyes down her long body, then back up to her face, which she'd smushed into the snow to be as small as possible around him. She felt his power so much more in this body. It vibrated through every cell and made the air she breathed heavy. It felt as if a truck was sitting on her chest.

Ronin ran his hand down her shoulder to her ribs. Felt good, so why was she scared?

Ronin, Ronin, powerful Ronin. With those bright gold eyes and golden hair falling forward. His slight smile, nearly hidden in his beard, the one he used to hide the scars on his neck from the world. Storm clouds above him made his skin look even paler, eyes look even brighter. He pulled off a leather necklace and his shirt. He stood smoothly and unbuckled his belt. Her ears perked at the jingle of the metal. What was he doing? He took out his chain wallet and unhooked it from his belt, then shoved his jeans down his legs. And before it even registered with her what he intended to do, Ronin Changed.

He. Changed.

Shit shit shit shit! As the massive lion slammed down to the snow on all fours, Emerald scrambled off. He had her pinned before she'd made it to the swing set. A snarl rattled his throat, and now she was going to die. She hissed. Ronin was huge, with a thick brown mane, fiery eyes, and black scars on his face. One of his ears had a huge notch ripped out of it. His paws on either side of her were the size of her whole head. How could a lion be this big? He settled his nose against her neck and inhaled deeply. She was so frozen, so terrified, she might as well have been the snow. Invisible. *Please don't hurt me.* Hiss.

When he set his teeth gently on her shoulder, she panicked. She didn't want to die. She reached out and swatted him, hooking her claws into his fur coat, right at his ribs. Another hiss.

He didn't even flinch. He let her claws stay right where they were and ran his long tongue up the side of her neck, over and over, until she retracted the claws from his hide. Her heart was going ninety-to-nothing, threatening to race out of her chest completely. Ronin laid half on top of her, one massive arm thrown over her body, pinning her down as he cleaned her slowly. Minutes drifted by, and still, he didn't kill her. He didn't even put her in her place. And eventually, she relaxed, muscle by muscle, and closed her eyes, enjoying the affection. Outside of her parents, had she ever experienced affection in this form? She couldn't remember. She remembered being a cub and getting clawed and bitten by the dominant cubs of the Pride. The only good memories she had in this form were the hours she'd spent alone in the woods, with no one there to scare her.

Ronin stood suddenly and made his way across the playground. Just...left.

Confused, Emerald sat up and watched him meander off. He was tricky. He walked slow and lazy, but she knew he could turn into a killer in no time flat. Still...she'd just been getting used to him, and now he was heading into the woods. Heading away from her.

She didn't like that.

Maybe she would just trail behind so she could see where he was going, but still be able to run away easily. Feeling like an escape artist genius, Emerald stood, twitched her tail, and then crunched through the snow after him. At the tree line, he slowed and came to a stop, then watched her over his shoulder.

Is he waiting for me? That's dangerous. Everything is dangerous.

She stopped, too.

He sat.

She sat.

They stared.

What now?

A roar sounded behind her and, on instinct, she bolted for Ronin. Hell no to getting eaten by a stranger lion! She would rather be eaten by him.

Ronin was standing now, looking at something behind her, and she skidded to a stop beside him. His ears were perked up, but his mouth was hanging open and he was panting slightly. Relaxed for the most part. Across the playground were a trio of adult male lions and one lioness.

Was it the Old Tarian Pride or the New Tarian Pride? From Ronin's reaction, she thought this was his Crew. He strode toward them, unhurried. Okay then. Emerald scampered behind him, dragging her belly through the snow, trailing just far enough back that he couldn't turn around and swat her. Not that he was showing any signs of aggression, but a wuss could never be too careful. She wanted to roll her eyes at herself, but again, the lioness controlled this body.

He ran his face down the side of the lioness first. Rose? It was probably Rose. She guessed so, since the lioness came straight over to Emerald and greeted her. Like a nice lioness. Like Rose had done. Emerald lay frozen in the snow like a fucking lion-cicle while Rose bumped her forehead against hers. The male lions approached slowly, bobbing their heads as they stared at Emerald.

This was her nightmare. They were all dominant brawlers, and now she was definitely going to die.

Ronin was larger than all of them and wary. He paced away and then back as the others approached closer to Emerald, step by tentative step. The lions seemed only curious, but Emerald wasn't used to Prides. She wasn't used to so many dominant lions around her at once, and she couldn't breathe. She rolled over on her side. *Please don't hurt me.*

One of the males was braver than the rest and sauntered up to her. He pushed his nose against her shoulder and then her neck. This was okay. He was just checking her out. Everything was okay. But when he placed his paw on her ribs and put pressure on her, Ronin snarled and swatted him right off her. The lion fell hard in the snow, and then Ronin herded him away aggressively. His body was tensed up, every powerful muscle rippling, the warning in his throat deafening. Rose laid beside her, tail twitching as she watched Ronin back the lion into a snowdrift. The other three males were inching away, tails down, ears flattened.

They all felt like Alphas, even the lioness beside her. These were the Tarians she remembered.

Emerald backed away, her belly making a trail in the snow. The three males bolted behind her, and now she was trapped between them and the fight. They had lowered to the ground stretched their necks forward, sniffing at her tail. Rose hissed but she didn't seem too bothered by them.

Suddenly, Ronin let off a *whoof* sound. It was a chuffing. He did it over and over, his rib muscles flexing with each call he gave. The others trotted away a few steps, ears erect, eyes on their Alpha. A lion roared in the woods, then another and another.

Ronin was calling them. Why? Emerald didn't want to do this. She didn't want to be in the middle of whatever was happening. Her submissiveness only set off dominants. It made them defensive. Her lying here in the snow like some dead thing made them instinctively want to fix her, like she was a wounded member of the pride. It made them want to fix her...or end her. She was confusing them all, like she always did, and confusion in lions led to aggression. Look at Ronin, charging the three males. Charging his own pride because of her. He was trying to protect her, but from what? His own people. Stupid lioness.

Ronin gave off three short roars again, and the other lions in the woods appeared in the clearing, trotting toward them. Was this the entire Pride here now? Rose arched her head back and roared, too, and the three closest to them joined in.

And what did Emerald do?

She laid there like a bump on a log.

And hated herself.

She had been born into this powerful body, but with a weak soul, and for what? What good did it do her? It only confused her and every shifter around her. She wrecked the balance.

Ronin herded the lions toward the old trail leading through the woods, leaving only her behind, and she understood. He'd told her before she didn't belong here. Her place was to stay invisible.

So she watched them all leave. And when Ronin turned around, she wished she could smile at him. *It's okay. I understand.*

But he trotted back to her and swatted her on the ass. Was this the part where she was going to die? No, he was trying to get her up.

Good luck, bucko, my lioness doesn't mind anyone— With a hiss, Emerald stood up and slunk beside him. And when he followed his Pride, she stayed right there at his side.

Well...this was new.

The Pride kept stopping and waiting, eyes on her, eyes on Ronin, back to her, back to Ronin.

Ronin was Alpha. He should've been in front, leading them all. But instead, he was walking slowly beside her. She didn't understand.

There was a soft rumbling every time Ronin exhaled a frozen breath, and every ten steps or so, he would swerve into her and rub his body down the side of hers. The first time he did it, she went to her belly. But he'd protected her. He hadn't hurt her. He was being patient and walking with her. So each time he moved toward her, she tried a little harder to stand her ground until her lioness rubbed her face against the side of his thick mane.

And inside, Emerald wanted to cry with happiness. Because she'd never been okay around other dominant lions, but Ronin made her feel safe. Who was going to mess with her when she was under his protection? No one. He was king here.

And the more she watched him, content to walk with her at the back of the Pride, the more she realized something.

An Alpha and a Pride were only as strong as the weakest member—and that would always be her. She was better off in Cassius's Pride where she could cause dissention in the ranks just by being herself.

She understood that, but as she walked through the snowy woods with these powerful animals, feeling like she was a part of something...she selfishly wanted to stay.

NINE

Why wouldn't her hands stop shaking? She tried twice to tie her boots, but she messed up the bow both times. She would probably never get used to Changing in front of people. The others had Changed back to their human forms, seemingly unaffected, like they did this all the time in front of each other, but for Emerald, it was different. Changing had always been a secretive thing in the years she'd been rogue with her family. She'd hid what she was, and taught her lioness to feel almost...ashamed. And realizing that made Emerald a little sad. She'd been part of making her lioness invisible without knowing it. She tried again to tie her shoe, but her silly trembling hands messed it all up again. She could feel everyone's attention on her.

"Here, let me," Ronin murmured, kneeling in front of her.

"Ronin, get up," she whispered. "You shouldn't be kneeling in front of me. You're Alpha."

"You don't really understand what being Alpha means, do you?" he murmured, frowning up at her as he finished tying her shoe. His eyes were still bright gold, and made her heartbeat stutter a bit.

She didn't understand what he meant, but before she could ask, a dark-haired man from Ronin's Crew, Kannon, he'd called him, strode by. He was bare-butt-naked and didn't cover his swinging dick at all. On a frozen breath, he muttered, "Yeah, well, you don't know what being Alpha means either, Ronin."

"What's that supposed to mean?" Ronin snarled, standing.

"It means we all know what you're going to do," he yelled, rounding on him. The man had fresh claw marks on his arms and ribs. Maybe he was one of the lions in the fight outside of the cabin earlier. "You'll leave us here and go guns a-blazing at Cassius alone. Right? Because of this girl?"

The others were gathering around now.

"It's not your fight," Ronin murmured.

"It is! You've made it our fight. We are backing you. We went against our friends and family to back you."

"And when it comes to fighting the Old Tarian Pride? Huh, Kannon? What will you do? How will you feel? Because we just had a meeting and you were all still sympathizing with them."

"Is it loyalty you're questioning?" Kannon growled, his eyes the color of sunlight. "Because if you're really questioning if we would have your back…then why the fuck are you here? Why the fuck did you take this throne?"

"He's…he's just taking me back to Cassius. Nothing more," Emerald said in a mouse-quiet voice.

"Oh, she speaks!"

"Careful," Ronin rumbled, tipping his chin back and looking down his straight nose at Kannon.

It was Rose who stepped in between the dominant lion shifters. "What Kannon is saying has merit. At some point, you're going to have to trust us. You can't fight a war all on your own. Cassius will win if we're weak, and what you're doing? Acting like you're still a rogue lion? It will make us all weak."

The others began to walk away, and Emerald could see it so clearly. There was a crack in this Pride the size of a canyon. On one side was the Alpha, and on the other were the rest of them.

"Can I make an observation?" she said as loud as she could. Only it came out a whisper.

When Ronin looked down at her, she wanted to hang her head, but there was no time for that. Standing, she clenched her fists and found her bravery. Louder, she asked, "Can I say something?"

The others slowed and turned. "Are you here to make judgements?" Kannon asked.

"N-no." She swallowed hard. "I have no right to judge anyone. I just wanted to point out that Ronin is trying to protect you." She shrugged. "I can see that clear as day, but you don't."

"Was he trying to protect us when he killed the Second of the Old Tarian Pride last night?" a tall man with a limp asked. "By himself?"

"Yeah, Gray," Ronin answered for her. "Do you want to know why?"

Gray frowned and shifted his weight to his sturdier leg. "Yeah, actually."

"Because," Ronin said, "my life is less important

than yours."

Rose frowned. "What?"

"You are the good that came from the Tarian Pride. You're the misfits. You could've joined in with every other fuckin' lion in existence and rebuilt a council immediately. But you...what, a dozen of you? Stood up to everyone. There is no council right now because you have been rallying against it. You were the ones who wanted change, and you didn't just sit by and let the same shit that's been happening for generations happen again. You stood up and said, 'That's enough.'" Ronin's smile was half wicked, half proud. "I just want to make sure you're ready before I ask you to fight the people who used to be in your Pride."

"They were in your Pride, too," Kannon pointed out.

Ronin growled softly.

"I think you should do team-building projects," Emerald suggested, hunkering down into her jacket as she made her way toward the others.

"Lady, we just Changed together. You can't get much more team-building than that." He held out his hand as she meandered closer. "I'm Terrence."

"Hi," she murmured, giving his hand a shake. "Emerald."

"We know," the man said with a chuckle. "We all remember you."

"You do?"

"Uh, yeah," Kannon murmured. "Why do you think we aren't over here screaming 'spy'? You hated this place as a cub."

"That, and you came in with a pretty gnarly shiner," Terrence said darkly. "Pretty sure you were dragged back to Old Tarian, and pretty sure you have every right to hate that Pride just as much as we do."

"What kind of team-building projects?" Ronin asked thoughtfully.

"Like, drinking together," Emerald said with a giggle.

"I'm in," Kannon said.

Ronin snorted. "You all are annoying enough without alcohol."

"But think about it," Emerald said. "The fastest way to bond with people is to make memories of doing stupid shit together."

"Thank you!" Kannon said, turning and holding his hands out. "I've been asking to get some fun up here for weeks. A cornhole game, Ouija board, something! I'm going stir-crazy. And none of us can leave because 'safety in numbers' and the Old Tarian Pride runs the town. It's go to work in town, be wary, come right back. Day after day, it's the same monotonous existence."

"So safety-in-numbers it and go to a bar in town together," Emerald suggested. "What's the Old Tarian Pride gonna do? Attack you in public?"

"Uh, yeah," Terrence murmured. "They don't give a fuck, and it's bad publicity on us if we go all murder-kitty on Main Street."

Ronin pushed a branch aside and let her pass. And when she did, he squeezed her ass gently and gave her a wink. She gasped a little, but the rest of the Pride didn't seem to notice as they walked in front, chattering about something called cornhole.

Emerald bumped his shoulder. "Can I ask you something?"

"Ask anything."

"I saw you last night. Hitting that shifter who hurt Rose. You didn't give a fuck either, and you don't strike me as the type of man who would prolong anything."

Ronin frowned. "I don't understand."

"I watched a man go in there guns a-blazin' with no one to back him up." She shrugged. "I don't understand why you're hesitating on this war."

He huffed a dark chuckle. "We already had the first battle."

"What?"

Ronin nodded. "How do you think I got the Old Tarians to leave this territory and set up the new one near town? They lost." His eyes darkened. "But so did we. One thing I didn't expect as a new Alpha was hurting when I lost some of the Pride. I barely knew them, but their loss weighs on me. It was my first time bonding to shifters, binding a Pride to me, and it was intense. And then a few days later, half of those bonds were broken."

"You lost half the Pride," she whispered.

Kannon turned and cast a sad look at her. "Feels like we lost more sometimes. We lost on their side, too."

"And the fact that you said 'we' right there is why I've been waiting until I know you are ready," Ronin said in a gritty voice as he stepped around a brush pile.

Terrence had been watching them. He'd been casting her and Ronin Sideways glances. "Speaking of needing allies—"

"We didn't speak of needing allies," Ronin said.

"We've all voted on two candidates for your mate," Terrence said, ignoring him.

Beside her, a wave of anger pulsed from Ronin and made Emerald's lioness shrink to almost nothing.

"We can discuss this later."

"Now's a good time," Terrence said softly, his narrowed eyes on Emerald. Whatever he was looking for on her face, she had no idea.

"Perhaps when we aren't in mixed company," Rose said firmly from up ahead.

Terrence ignored them. "Our first choice is Aria Dunn and second is Blakely Winters of the Deadlies Pride."

The woods grew silent except for the crunching of their steps in the snow and the soft snarl rattling Ronin's throat.

"Blakely is a blond," Terrence continued. "Tall. Nice rack—"

Ronin slammed him against a tree so hard it shook snow in the upper branches. "I said not now."

"Why?" Terrence snarled. "Because Cassius's mate has your attention? She's off-limits and gives no benefit to us. You say we're more important than you? Act like it."

Suddenly, Emerald was homesick. Not for a place, but for her old life where everything made sense.

She didn't belong anywhere.

It felt as if she was some star way up in the sky, orbiting a great story she was watching unfold on Earth, but she wasn't a part of it. Not really. She was just a witness.

"I'll help however I can," she said to no one in particular.

Ronin cast her a look over his shoulder and pushed off Terrence. "What do you mean?"

"Terrence was right. I have just as much right as anyone to hate the Old Tarian Pride." She forced a smile. "I can't imagine females last too long under Cassius. But while I'm there, I'll be your little grenade on the inside of his Pride. After my dad is safe, I'll do what I can for you."

"Why would you do that?" Kannon asked in the silence of the still woods.

Ronin's words had stuck with her. Sometimes a

life was just a life with no big destiny, no big meaning. It was just birth, the middle stuff, and then death. She'd never felt like she was meant for anything. Her whole life's focus had been hiding from the Tarian Pride, and look where she was now? Headed right back into the heart of it. She'd utterly failed at escaping. But these people, these outcasts, they were trying to change the fate of an entire Pride that had been poisoned with evil for generations. They were trying to save this Pride, to rehabilitate it, and to save who-knows-how-many lives from them in the future. They'd been raised in hate, every one of them, but here they were trying to do good.

Ronin was right.

They were important.

So she lifted her chin in the air because she was determined to be stronger, and uttered his same words. "Because my life is less important than yours."

TEN

Hearing those words fall from her lips hurt Ronin's chest in ways he couldn't understand. How could she think her life was less valuable? He was an Alpha. A good Alpha knew the power of his Pride was in the comfort of its members. If they were okay, he was doing all right as their leader. But Emerald? Thinking she was less valuable? Now nothing in him wanted to return her to Cassius. She would take unnecessary risks if she thought it would help Ronin's Pride.

And that spoke volumes of the woman she was.

But it also scared him because, after today, she mattered very, very much to him. His inner lion couldn't take his attention away from her for even a second.

Beautiful Emerald. She was tough. Tougher than she gave herself credit for. And selfless.

Her dad had told her to run, and here she was, climbing into the cab of Ronin's truck, somber and quiet, but with a determined set to her mouth. How many people would've saved themselves instead of trading themselves for someone they cared for?

He buckled her in. Did she need him to? Fuck no, she could take care of herself, but he wanted the excuse to lean over her lap and steal one last kiss. He let his lips linger on hers. They were late to the meeting with Cassius, but he was finding it hard to care.

She tasted so sweet. Like the honey she'd just smeared on her toast a few minutes ago. She hadn't been hungry for the huge meal he'd brought to the park, but she'd agreed to him making her a piece of honey toast before she went back to the Old Tarian Pride.

Her eyes had little blue specks when he studied them up close like this. Had anyone else ever noticed? He hoped not. He hoped he was the only one who knew about the blue. "I wish…" *You could be mine. I could take you out. I could make you queen. I could protect you. I could fix this fucked-up situation we're in. I wish you could stay here with me.*

"I know," she murmured. Her lip trembled. and she bit down and then forced a little smile. Brave Em.

She didn't know it yet, but he was going to figure out a way to go back for her after her father was safe. He wished he would've known last night, and he would've rescued him, too. Now, the Old Tarian Pride would be ready for a rescue mission, and that put her dad in even more danger. He wasn't going to worry her with that knowledge, though.

"Hand me your phone."

Emerald put her hand on her chest dramatically and inhaled. "Are you asking for my number?"

Ronin chuckled. "I'm giving you mine." He punched it in and sent a text to himself. "And now I have your number."

Before she could say anything clever, he inhaled deeply and shut the passenger door, strode around the front, frozen air chugging in front of him. He slid in behind the wheel and sighed, gripping the steering wheel. "Zeke always told me if you like a woman, don't beat around the bush about it. Let her know.

There's my number," he said, flickering his fingers toward her phone. "I want to talk to you again. I like you." He nodded once and held her pretty green gaze. "Now you know."

And he got to see it there. She melted. Her eyes went all soft, and her smile turned tender and her cheeks turned the prettiest shade of pink. God, she was a stunner.

"I like you, too. I thought I should say that now, just in case…"

"You'll see me again, Em. I swear it on my life."

Her smile turned so sad it hollowed out his chest. "And if I see you again, I'll be an Old Tarian queen, and you'll be paired up. You'll be an amazing mate for one of those strangers, and I'll have to smile at you and pretend I'm okay."

Ronin shook his head and stared out the front window of the woods. He squeezed her thigh. "Em, the only seer I ever knew was named Beaston. You ain't him. You can't see what the future will be like. Everything will be okay. I'll fix it." He edited his number in her phone and entered his name as Jenny. When she frowned at it, he grinned and handed it back to her. "In case the Pride watches your phone."

"Very clever," she said with a tinkling giggle. Good God, he hoped he could hear that laugh again soon. It was infectious.

He started the truck. "Just so you know," he said over the sound of the engine roaring to life, "the Pride doesn't Change together very much."

Emerald tucked her legs under her and rested her cheek against the seat. "What do you mean?"

Ronin hit the gas and eased onto the road that led away from the cabin. "I mean you attracted them. Something about you. Something good. We've been pretty stale and frustrated around here, but today was different. You're a bright spot, Em."

"Me?" she asked softly. Why were her eyes so hopeful? Did she really not understand how special she was? "Well...Terrence doesn't like me."

Ronin snorted. "Terrence can eat a dick. He just wants me to focus on my duties."

Emerald snorted, and he could've sworn she murmured, "You said doody."

He was about to laugh, but movement in the rearview caught his attention. Kannon was pulling up behind them, driving his old rusted-out, beat-up Bronco. "What the hell?" he muttered, slowing down.

He began rolling down his window to tell all the lions piled in Kannon's rig to "piss off," but Emerald slid her hand over his leg and stopped him. "They're being a good Pride, having their Alpha's back. They choose to be here, Ronin. Let them."

She was right. Smart kitty. He was being too careful trying to protect everyone and was stunting their ability to bond as a Pride.

Emerald was texting someone on her phone as he pulled through the security checkpoint. Gray was working it today.

"Anything?" Ronin asked Gray.

"Not a peep," he murmured. " I keep doing perimeter searches, and I'm watching the monitors like a hawk, but nothing. Birds aren't even setting off the motion sensors today. It's too quiet." He cast a frown at the Bronco behind him. "Is everyone going to the drop-off?"

"None of them are," Emerald said suddenly. She shoved open her door and turned. "It was nice to meet you, Ronin. I hope to see you again someday." The way she spoke was so formal, as if she'd already shut down.

"What are you doing?" he asked.

"I'm protecting you." She lifted her chin higher. "You and I both know they're waiting somewhere close. I've texted Derek that I'm headed toward them and to pick me up."

"It's freezing, Em. Get back in the truck."

"This is my choice." She moved to shut the door but hesitated. Her eyes roiling with determination, she told him, "Thank you. For today. It's a memory they can't take away from me." She ghosted him a sad smile and said it again, "This is my choice."

She shut the door and made her way on the snowy road past the fence. And this memory right here would be one he would never forget for the rest of his life.

A determined lioness with a protective streak a mile wide, walking a snowy road alone to an uncertain future.

"I should follow her, right?" he asked Gray.

"No," Gray rumbled. "She made her choice, and look." He turned one of the video monitors toward Ronin. Half a mile down the road, a black snowmobile was speeding toward them. It was dragging something heavy through the snow. Ronin squinted his eyes, but the snow was creating a rooster tail over whatever was tied behind.

"That's Derek driving," Gray murmured, biting his thumbnail as he studied the screen.

"Hmm," Ronin muttered, shoving open the door. Why wasn't Cassius here to pick up Emerald himself?

"Em!" he called, jogging after her, but she'd made ground. She was running toward the snowmobile at full speed, screaming something he couldn't understand.

"Aw, fuck!" Gray yelled. "Ronin! Derek's dragging a body!"

ELEVEN

Emerald could tell it was her father way before she got a clear view of him. Derek's smile gave it away. "Stop! Stop!" she shrieked, sprinting for the snowmobile that was blasting toward her, spewing snow on both sides. "You're hurting him!"

Please don't let him be dead. Please, God, don't let him be dead.

Her legs burned from running, and every muscle in her body was protesting the cold and the strain, but she didn't care. Nothing mattered except for Derek stopping his damn snowmobile. He was playing chicken, his laughter echoing through the mountains. He wasn't slowing down at all.

Tears blurred her vision, and a snarl ripped

through her chest. She hated him. She hated all of the Old Tarian Pride. Hated that they thought they could take whatever they wanted and hurt whoever got in their way.

Something broke inside of her as she watched the snow trailing from the blades of the snowmobile onto her limp and lifeless father. Something awful happened to her. Something that hurt. Maybe her heart was breaking.

Closer and closer, Derek rode until she could smell the stink of blood and oil. She wasn't going to slow down. Her fury wouldn't allow it. She leaped right as Derek was feet away from clipping her legs out from under her. She catapulted through the air and slammed into him hard, held on and tucked her thumb like Ronin and showed her and hit him as hard as she could. The crack of his nose rattled up her fist and through her entire body. The force hurt her hand and took the wind from her lungs for a moment.

Derek shoved her off of him by her neck, and she hit the ice hard and skidded several yards before she came to a stop. Heart pounding, she forced herself up, ignoring the pain in her shoulder from when she'd hit the ground, and ran for the slowing snowmobile the instant the traction on her boots allowed.

Derek came to a stop, and sobbing, Emerald skidded on her knees the last few feet to her father's limp body. He was blue, frozen straight through. She patted his cheeks and whispered frantically. "Dad? Dad wake up. I'm here." She looked up the road. Derek was coming for her, dismounting off the snowmobile, but she didn't care what he did to her. "Ronin!" she screamed. "Help!"

"You broke my fucking nose, you bitch!" Derek snarled, cupping his hands over his face. Red streamed down his chin.

Ronin's lion was coming. He was Changed and leading the Pride at a full sprint right for her.

"Dad? Dad, it's okay," she said, wiping snow from his face and silver hair. She cradled his head and put her cheek near his mouth, but she couldn't tell if he was breathing. His face was one big bruise.

"I'm going to kill you," she promised Derek, frantically untying the rope from her father's wrists. "It'll be my greatest accomplishment when I rid the world of your worthless—"

The click of metal on metal echoed through her head. When she looked up, Derek was aiming a handgun at her father's head.

"Get on the back, or I will pull this trigger. Now!"

Her eyes burned as time slowed. The New Tarian Pride was almost here, but Derek was putting pressure on that trigger with his finger.

"Don't, don't!" she cried. "I'll go. I'll go!"

"Now!" he screamed, his face going red, his veins popping.

Thank God, she'd already untied her father. She scrambled on, Derek's hand rough on the back of her neck, and then they were fishtailing out of there. She couldn't take her eyes off Dad's body as they did a U-turn and passed him by. Ronin was coming. He was coming. *Hold on, Dad.* He could help. *Please, let there be time for Ronin to help.* The metal of the gun was cold against her temple. She wanted to turn and see how close the lions were. They had to be so close. She could feel them. Hear them snarling. But she couldn't move. Derek would pull the trigger and not care.

Please let him live.

The deafening roars that grew quieter behind them, drowned out by the engine of the speeding snowmobile, told her that she was really on her own now.

Cheeks stained with weakness, she gritted her teeth and stared ahead at the road blurring under the blades of the snowmobile. They were going so fast, the old her would've been scared, but inside of her, the lioness didn't feel fear. For once, she wasn't shrinking, and she sure as fuck wasn't hiding.

She was planning.

Emerald didn't know how she was going to do it, but she was going to annihilate the Old Tarian Pride for what they'd done.

The lioness wasn't Invisible anymore.

Now, she was Fury.

TWELVE

He's alive.

Those were the two most important words she'd ever read in a text. It was the most meaningful word combination of her entire existence.

She wanted to write back to Jenny, aka Ronin, to please take care of him, but a man with platinum blond hair and striking blue eyes yanked the phone out of her hand and tossed it in the tote with her necklace and Emerald's ring that her mother had given her on her twenty-first birthday. He'd already patted her down in front of all of the Old Tarian Pride females, including Annamora, who hadn't looked up from the ground the entire time they'd been in the cabin. There were seven women here, sitting on the couch, on the arms of the couch, on a couple of chairs. Brunettes, blonds, redheads, they all wore the same somber expressions, and each face looked like the next. No one spoke except for the platinum blond man, who'd introduced himself as Orion. His introduction alone had surprised her. And he didn't particularly look like he was enjoying taking her possessions.

"It's not so bad here," he murmured. "So long as you mind the rules." He was speaking toward the floor, tucking her jacket into the bag.

Emerald glanced up at the video camera in the top corner of the den. This place was like a freaking cult. "What rules?" she asked, just as softly.

"No phones. No back-talk. Say yes to the males here and don't piss 'em off."

Annamora glanced up at him, and Emerald saw it there. A raw openness she didn't understand. She swallowed hard and looked down at the ground again. And as soft as a breeze, she whispered, "Orion can't keep you safe if you don't mind the rules."

Huh. Not that she trusted anyone here as far as she could throw them, but she asked Orion, "Do you know Ronin?"

The giant shrugged. "I'm not from here. I know *of* him. He's a traitor lion, switched alliances and grew up a tiger."

"He didn't have a choice—"

"Repeat the rules back," Orion growled, his eyes blazing such a light blue, they were the color of snow.

Emerald held his gaze a couple of seconds and then averted her own. "No phones. No talking back. Say yes."

"Good." Orion inhaled deeply and tossed Annamora a worried look. "Cassius isn't here right now."

Relief washed over Emerald like a tidal wave. If he wasn't here, there would be no ceremony today. She released a long breath and then asked, "Where is he?"

"Rule number four, stop asking all these damn questions." He jerked his chin toward the door. "Everyone out, go get dinner on and settle the boys down. And for fuck's sake, I don't want a repeat of the last two nights, just...be good. Annamora, you stay here with Emerald. Get her cleaned up. You have half an hour."

The two of them exchanged a look Emerald didn't

understand, and then he disappeared out the door saying, "I'll be right outside so don't try nothin'."

Annamora stood immediately and guided Emerald to a small love seat. She grabbed a brush from the table and started combing out the snarls, her back to the camera. "You look tired and like you've been crying," Annamora breathed out. "What happened?"

Unable to trust anyone here, Emerald said simply, "Ronin took me after I passed out."

"What's it like over there?"

Oh, no. She wasn't telling these Old Tarians shit. "Orion protects the girls?"

"As best he can. He ain't like the others. He's only here because his sister, Sora, is one of the queens. He's gentle when he's able, but when he's in front of the males? Well...you'll see. He has to do what he has to do to make sure he stays our guard. There isn't volume on the camera, by the way. They got security here, but we aren't rolling in the dough like the New Tarians. They're sittin' on a pile of investment money up there from our productive days. We used to pool our income and invest like crazy. Had a good finance team. Tarians weren't just the big Pride because we were monsters. We had even more power than that. We had numbers and we had assets, but we lost most of the money when we got chased out of that territory. We don't trust those human banks, so it was buried up in the old cemetery and guarded twenty-four-seven. Derek snuck out there to steal it when we first lost the territory, but the New Tarians are smart. They'd already moved it somewhere he couldn't find it." Suddenly she paused her brushing and asked, "Did the New Tarians hurt you?"

"No," Emerald murmured, brushing her fingertips against her lips just to remind herself of the last time Ronin had kissed her in the front seat of his truck. "They did the opposite."

Annamora sighed. "Well, they didn't do you any favors. You probably got spoiled, and now you'll have to adjust even more to life here. You smell like another male. You'll set off the Pride if you go to a meeting smelling like Ronin." She stood and then disappeared into a bathroom in the hallway, and a few seconds later, Emerald could hear the sound of shower water. Annamora returned and shooed her into the bath. And as she helped her undress—a very awkward situation for two strangers—Annamora's lips barely moved as she whispered, "Orion's makin' sure Derek stays away from you. That's why he's posted up outside. Derek is making it real obvious he hates you, and that's bad. Pretty Emerald, you made a dangerous enemy in that man. Ronin killed Dalt, and now Derek is Second. He's almost as bad as Cassius. Be wary around him, okay? Don't provoke him. You need to fit in here perfectly for a while, like a puzzle piece. Make people want to stick up for you. Trust me," she said, raising her delicately arched eyebrows high. "You don't want to be alone here."

"Why did you come here?" she asked before she stepped into the shower.

"What do you mean?"

"Why did you stay with this half of the Pride?"

Annamora shrugged up one shoulder and had the saddest set to her mouth when she murmured, "None of the girls here had a choice. Same as you."

And as the blonde left the room, Emerald was overwhelmed with sadness. *Same as you.*

That wasn't right, though. It wasn't fair. It wasn't okay to get bullied by chauvinistic males and pigeonholed into a shitty life just because they weren't seen as important. Males here had won the lottery because they were born dominant, and with a dick. Well, fuck their dicks and fuck their dominance.

"Annamora?" she asked just as the girl hit the hallway.

Annamora peeked her head back in. "Yeah? Do you need something?"

"Yes, I need something. I need you to be ready."

"For what?"

"I'm going to get us out of here."

It was a test. Her reaction would tell Emerald whether she passed or failed, because for all of her lioness's faults, she was a fantastic judge of character and honesty.

Annamora dropped her gaze, frowning at the tiles on the bathroom floor. But a second later she huffed a breath and lifted gold eyes to Emerald. "Is it better over there?" she whispered.

Emerald nodded.

Her throat moved as she swallowed, and her voice shook only a little when she said, "Then okay."

Emerald let Annamora's agreeance wash right through her instincts, and the lioness approved.

Brave Annamora, every bit as submissive as Emerald, and every bit as tired of the hand she'd been dealt.

It didn't matter how broken a person became. If they got pushed hard enough, that relentless pressure would create a window of opportunity. A chance to grow. To change. To become stronger. To become unbreakable.

Emerald had made a promise to herself when Annamora had helped her before that she would repay her. And she would—with a better life. Somehow.

Her mind raced through her quick shower, and she dressed in a hurry. No make-up because she didn't care what anyone thought of her here, and she towel-dried her hair as best she could before following a fidgeting Annamora out of the cabin and down the row of one-room cabins to the big house at the front of the territory.

"The other girls are already inside," Orion enlightened them as they climbed the porch stairs. Derek was waiting on the porch, leaning on the railing, his gold eyes narrowed and tracking Emerald's every moment. She'd never felt so hunted as she did under his gaze. It made her stomach churn. "Your nose is crooked," she observed. "I gave your face some character. You're welcome."

Derek didn't say a word, just tracked her with his gaze as she made her way inside. His empty smile made her skin crawl.

She missed Ronin. And not just the safety he enveloped her with, but...Ronin himself. She closed her eyes for a second and imagined his lips on hers. She then steeled herself and pushed her way through the crowd gathered in the living room. There were towering lion shifters everywhere. There were so many dominants in one room, she fought the old urge to run. To hide. To be invisible.

Hurt them back.

If she hadn't been here before, she wouldn't have known where the kitchen was. There were that many Pride members here. "Excuse me," she muttered, pushing past a trio of giants who purposely blocked her path.

Her politeness didn't move them. Instead, they clumped closer together and glared down at her with the devil himself in their smiles. More of them gathered behind her, blocking off her view of Annamora. Emerald's lioness didn't like being separated from her friend, and a growl rattled her chest.

"Your face looks all healed up," one of them said. "I can't decide if you look prettier with a shiner or not. What do you think, Carl?"

The Carl in question walked around her, and for a split second, she could see Annamora. One of the males was holding her in place by the back of the neck, and she was giving Emerald a warning look. *Careful.*

"She belongs to Cassius," Orion growled.

"Shut the fuck up," Carl said, lurching at Orion.

And Orion, to his credit, didn't back down an inch. He stood up straighter and his eyes blazed white as he glared down Carl-the-megachode.

"You got the balls to post up?" Carl scoffed. "What's your job here, Orion? To wrangle a bunch of scatterbrained women? You're a glorified babysitter, not a guard."

"I'd rather be a glorified babysitter than a goat-licking douchetart, Carl."

"Oh, shit," Emerald murmured. Her eyebrows were so far up in her hairline, her forehead ached.

"You really want to do this?" Carl yelled.

"Been waiting my whole fuckin' life," Orion said

with a grim smile. His eyes flickered to Annamora. "Get her out of here," he gritted out as he turned to lead the trio of giant assholes out the front door.

By "get her out of here," Emerald honestly couldn't tell if he meant out of the living room or out of the territory. Orion was confusing.

"He'll be fine," Annamora whispered, grabbing her by the hand and yanking her toward the kitchen.

"H-how do you know?" Emerald asked, watching the four behemoths shoving their way through the front door.

"Trust me," Annamora said. "They're barking up the wrong tree with Orion. They keep testing him because he ain't from here, but they keep coming back with their skulls nearly bashed in. And no one's got him pissed off enough to Change yet. He's been beating them fist to fist, but you can just tell his animal is a monster. Probably got white eyes and looks like a damn demon…"

Someone suddenly grabbed the back of Emerald's hair and shoved her forward, then released her so she blasted toward the kitchen island. She barely caught herself before her nose hit the hard edge. Chest heaving, she turned slowly to find Derek chuckling to himself and stalking toward her slowly. "That was close," he murmured.

"Cassius won't like your hands on me," Emerald said, straightening her spine.

"Cassius won't give a shit. It was supposed to be your pairing day, and where is he?" Derek looked around at the jeering males around him. "Are you Cassius?" he asked one of them.

"Not I," said the monster.

"You?" he asked another.

The man with a scar down his face and only one eye looked her up and down and said, "I wish."

"This ain't just a meeting, cupcake. This was supposed to be your celebration. Your coronation. You were supposed to be one of *them* already." He gestured to the blonde, Sora, and the two brunettes who had been serving Cassius when she'd come here. The other mates.

She let herself get lost in a merry-go-round memory. She was scared, and sometimes it was easier to escape to a pretty picture in her head than face reality. She was new to this bravery thing, and it was a lot with all this attention on her. The memory didn't hold though. It was a kiss from Ronin and then the vision flickered and faded. Dominants were everywhere, and they all looked hungry. For her. It felt like bugs were crawling under her skin, and she wanted to retch as Derek brushed her hair off her shoulders. She leaned back away from him as far as she could, but the countertop was blocking any escape.

Trapped. Trapped. Trapped.

"Hey, man, leave her alone," one of the males said from the crowd.

Derek rounded on an unfamiliar man and snarled, "Or what, Cason?"

The man dropped his head to the side, but his eyes were full of anger. His gaze flickered to Emerald, and he twitched his chin toward the other side of the kitchen.

Okay then. Emerald sidestepped to the other females, who had stopped their meal preparations and were staring leerily at Derek. One of the mates of Cassius, the submissive blond one, brushed her fingertips against Emerald's back and then held her shirt gently to keep her in place. "Stay in the middle of us tonight," she whispered shakily.

Oooooh, something was happening. There was a

tension here that she didn't understand. Dissention in the ranks. A Pride wasn't supposed to squabble like this. She was beginning to think that not all of the Old Tarians were bad. Perhaps they'd just gotten stuck in a situation they couldn't escape. Like her.

The saying that it took one bad apple to ruin the bunch? Well, what if here it took a few *good* apples to ruin the Old Tarian Pride? They could ruin them with morals.

Hope fluttered in her chest. She wished for the hundredth time today that Ronin was here and she wasn't navigating this alone, but maybe this was meant to be. She'd always believed that some people's destinies were beige. They weren't meant for anything exciting, weren't meant to make a ripple in the ocean of their generation. She'd always thought that was her, but now...she felt something building, something growing, some storm that was much bigger than her, and she was right in the eye of it. And her lioness, the Fury now, was watching and waiting like a wild lion in hip-high grass, the same color of her fur, every muscle tensed, eyes steady on some prey Emerald couldn't figure out yet.

Derek turned around to find her gone from where

he'd cornered her. Emerald smiled at him. She shouldn't poke at the rattlesnake, but today she couldn't seem to help herself. He'd hurt her dad. She would never forget him dragging Dad behind that snowmobile while he laughed.

She'd never been able to hold a dominant's gaze before today.

Something had really broken inside of her.

Or maybe Ronin had put her together, she didn't know.

Hurt them back.

"What can I do to help?" she asked the girl with the hand gripping Emerald's shirt.

The woman, Sora, rested her forehead between Emerald's shoulder blades and released a shuddering breath. And on that breath, she whispered, "When you run, I want to come, too."

"Me, too," a brunette mouthed quickly before she returned to buttering loaves of French bread.

Hurt them back.

Females were power to a Pride, right? That's why Cassius was binding mates to him. If they paired up, their families became allies. Well, if Emerald took the Old Tarian females, where would that leave this

Pride?

Hurt them back.

It would leave them without allies and with a big gaping hole for Ronin and his people to come in and destroy this Pride from the inside out.

She turned and squeezed the girl's hand gently and gave her a single nod. *Okay. Let's hurt them back.*

And inside of her, for the first time since the lioness had been broken…or had awoken…Fury smiled.

THIRTEEN

"Can you hear that?" Annamora whispered in the dark. "Something's happening."

The room didn't have any windows. Just cots lined up and thin blankets to cover them in the frosty night.

Emerald was wearing the clothes she'd worn to the Pride meeting—to stay warm, yes, but also to stay ready. Because Annamora was right. There was lots of activity and talking right outside. This cabin was located near the big house, but a much smaller version. Cassius's two brunette mates were missing, but Annamora had explained they were waiting in the big house for Cassius to come home from some super-secret meeting that had the entire Pride all abuzz.

Whatever his meeting was for, Emerald was eternally grateful, because she sure as heck hadn't wanted to have a pairing day with him. His duties had bought her time.

Ha! Doodies. It shouldn't be funny right now, but doodie was and always would be her favorite word.

"We have to be careful," Maris, one of the females murmured as Emerald stood and pressed her ear against the wall. "If they come in here and we're out of bed, they will punish us. I'll tell you when they're coming." She scrambled out of her tangled sheets and pressed her ear against the door.

Annamora hopped up, too, and tiptoed to the wall right beside her. She pulled a glass off the nightstand beside her and pressed it to the wall, then pushed her ear onto the bottom like some old spy movie. Emerald snorted at the very very serious look on Annamora's face.

"Not funny," her new friend said. "I'm a professional detective."

"Oh, are you?"

Annamora grinned and held up Emerald's cell phone, and in the dim light, she waggled her eyebrows.

"Oh my gosh!" Emerald whisper-screamed.

"It's been going off for a while. Jenny is very persistent." Annamora checked the door. "It took three of us casually searching the house to figure out where Orion kept it."

"Be quieter," one of the girls murmured from the cots behind them.

"All I hear is mumbling." Annamora pouted out her bottom lip and replaced the glass on the table. "Is Jenny-texts-a-lot really Ronin?"

Emerald snorted as she opened his texts.

Em? Can you just tell me you're okay? I'm going insane.

Two hours later:

Something big is happening, can you get to a safe place? Away from everyone?

Em? Fuck, I need to know you're out of the way.

Fifteen minutes ago:

We're here.

"Oh, nooo!" Now was the time for panic.

"What?" Annamora asked.

Should she tell them? Should she trust these Old Tarian lionesses, sitting up in their cots and staring at her with glowing eyes as round as dinner plates? What was the right decision here?

"Someone's coming!" Maris whispered, running toward her cot.

Shit! Emerald dove for her own cot, and she and Annamora both threw their covers over them. And right before the door opened, Emerald shoved the cell phone under her arm and closed her eyes. Her heart was pounding so hard as the door creaked open. She didn't dare open her eyes, but she heard him. Heard the footsteps on the floor as he walked along the feet of their cots. She inhaled, but she couldn't tell who it was. Not Derek and not Orion. And not Ronin. Those, she had memorized.

The clomping boot steps faded away, hesitated at the door, and then the door clicked closed. Something felt off, though. The air still felt too heavy, so she kept perfectly still, kept her eyes closed, slowed her breathing.

Her lioness had pinpointed the exact spot in the room where he was. She could feel him watching her. A soft snarl rattled up her throat before she could stop it.

"You feel different," Cassius rumbled.

Not being able to see him was the worst part, so she opened her eyes.

"So green. I wonder will you give our cubs those eyes of yours?" Cassius was crouched in the corner, elbows on his knees. It was dark in here, so all she could see was the outline of his form and his glowing gold eyes.

"Could you be any creepier?" she asked. Okay, she didn't even understand where she'd gotten the courage to talk to him like this. Something was really wrong with her lioness.

The phone vibrated against her arm, and she hugged it closer to stifle the sound.

Cassius stood and flicked on the light switch. Emerald winced and blinked hard, wishing her eyes would adjust fast.

"Listen to that heartbeat race," he murmured.

"Mmmm, the answer is yes then. You *can* get creepier."

"Keep it up, bitch. You're just making my blood boil." He canted his head the other way, narrowing his eyes on her. "You are much more interesting than you were before. I assumed you were a mouse, but you don't feel like a mouse. Your face looks better.

Quick healer." Why did he sound so suspicious? He walked over to her and dragged his gaze down her body. Kneeling slowly, he murmured, "I think you will be very fun to break."

Emerald didn't even try to stop the snarl in her throat. She offered him an empty smile to match his. "I think you already did."

"Hmmm." He leaned forward and parted his lips to say something more, but the door opened.

"The rest of the council is asking to see you," Orion murmured. He looked as pale as a ghost, and his nearly-white gaze flickered to Emerald, and then back to his Alpha.

In disbelief at what Orion had just said, she asked, "The council?" *Please let there be some mistake.*

The soulless smile stretched across Cassius's entire face. "Take heart, my queen. Not only have you landed yourself the most powerful Alpha, but I'm the head of the new council as well."

No combination of words had ever made her feel quite as sick as those. "No," she uttered in horror.

"As of today, the council is complete and in charge of the lion shifters again. First order of business is to annihilate the weak Alpha who took you from me and killed my Second." His voice was a gritty snarl, and his eyes swam with insanity. "Ronin dies tonight, along with every member of his Pride who fought against me." And as he stood and walked away, his voice echoed behind him. "I win."

Emerald laid there frozen as Orion closed the door.

"Oh my gosh, oh my gosh," Annamora whispered.

"This is really bad!" another of the lionesses whispered, sitting up.

"What do we do?" Annamora asked. "If they snuff out the New Tarian Pride, we are all stuck. There will be nowhere for us to run!"

Fingers flying, Emerald typed out, *Ronin, I'm fine. I'm fine!!! Run and hide!* Send.

Two seconds went by with no answer, and it was too much.

You can't be here. Send.

The council is back. Send.

Cassius leads them. Send.

They'll kill you! Send.

The only answer was a sudden yelling and chaos outside.

And then the cabin rattled with the roaring of the

lions.

Emerald bolted for the door, but it was locked. She yanked on the doorknob so hard it broke off. So she put her fingers through the hole she'd made, rested the sole of her foot against the wall, and yanked at the door. It splintered.

"What do we do?"

"You stay here or you fight," Emerald said, just as the door gave way and came flying inward. Huffing breath, she rounded on the girls. "You want a better life? You protect the ones who can give that to you. If you are fine being treated like the shit on their shoes here? Then you stay in this room and do nothing. We always have a choice! The Old Tarians tried to convince us we don't, but we do. And tonight, that's your choice. Pick a Pride. Choose wisely because your quality of life depends on it."

The girls looked terrified. These weren't Old Tarian warrior lionesses. The dominants here had been replacing them gradually with females who were submissive, who they could control. These weren't fighters. But they'd asked what to do, and the rest was up to them.

Annamora and Sora stepped forward at the same

time. Tears were staining Sora's cheeks, but she lifted her chin primly and said, "Orion, get out of the way."

It was then that Emerald felt it—the heaviness behind her. She turned to find the platinum blond man with the scary ice-colored eyes glaring at her, his lip snarled up, and his canines too long. Too sharp.

"Sora—"

"I cannot be treated like this and survive. I choose to survive."

"Me, too," Annamora rushed out.

He looked at Emerald, who shrugged and said, "I'm mostly here to fuck shit up."

One of the girls snorted behind her, but she didn't know who because, currently, she was blowing right past a growly Orion and sprinting for the front of the house. Inside of her, Fury, as her lioness had apparently deemed herself, was ready, waiting for the signal to take her skin. She needed logic, though, first.

Step one: Find Ronin.

Step two: Save Ronin.

Step three: Bone Ronin.

Step Four: Have, like, seven baby Ronins.

Step Five: —

Ack! An impossibly strong hand went around her throat and forced her through the open doorway and out onto the porch. The edges of her vision blurred as Derek pulled her to him. His breath was hot on her face when he asked, "What the fuck have you done?"

"Nothing...yet," she choked out, gripping his wrists, trying desperately to pry him off. She couldn't breathe!

Ronin's voice was in her head. *Fight dirty*.

Emerald took her hands from his wrists, grabbed his shoulders and slammed her knee upward into his fragile little ball sack as hard as she possibly could.

The whoosh of air from his lungs and the creaking high-pitched grunt he made would've been funny if he still didn't have his hands around her throat. Emerald made a fist like Ronin taught her and blasted him against the jaw before he recovered. Again and again until his hands loosened on her neck and he fell backward over the porch railing. In the halos of light between the big house and this one, there was war. Lions were engaged in an all-out to-the-death brawl. She couldn't tell who was New and who was Old Tarian Pride, but her heart stuttered in her chest when she saw him—Ronin. Her Ronin, because that's what he'd always been. Her hero. The one she'd remembered all this time for his kindness. He was hers, there when she needed someone to step in. To step up. To stand up…for her. For what was right.

He came out of the shadowy woods, jeans slung low, rage in his blazing eyes as he strode toward Cassius, fists clenched, blond hair disheveled, his face twisted into something not quite human. He felt so heavy he filled the entire clearing. Stunned, she watched as Cassius roared an inhuman sound from the other side of the clearing. The chaos of war around them didn't matter. They were only focused on each other. Cassius, big, dark, soulless Alpha intent on bending people to his will. Ronin, light, strong, steady, protective, knew the value of every Pride member…she'd never witnessed a fight between good and evil like this.

Ronin's speed as he bolted for Cassius stole her breath away. And as he launched himself through the air, his lion ripped out of him and clashed so violently against Cassius's animal, she felt the power of their hatred in her chest. She gasped at the raw brutality of their fight—two titans latched onto each other with their claws. Ronin raked his weapons across Cassius's skin, sank his teeth into him, slapped those monstrous paws against the dark Alpha. Their paws dragged long tread marks through the snow, exposing the black earth underneath like some Jackson Pollok painting. In moments, of the snow was speckled and splattered in red.

Motion caught her attention. As she watched a dozen more lions charging from the shadows, barreling straight for the Alpha fight, she chanted under her shaking breath, "no, no, no." Some deep instinct told her they weren't friends. The scarred-up monsters were the new council, here to protect their alliances, here to defend their new throne.

Old Tarians didn't fight with honor.

Rage pulsed through her veins. *Now?* Fury asked inside of her.

"Now," she gritted out, sprinting down the steps and into the yard. She let the lioness have her. This wouldn't be like every other Change. This would be a broken lioness who didn't have a single thing to lose anymore.

The pain was blinding as the animal tore out of her. She didn't mean for the scream in her throat to escape. She wanted to be tough like all the badass males who were locked in battle around her. Bowed on the ground, on all fours, her Change lasted eternal seconds, and the pained sound in her throat evolved. It turned into a sound she'd never heard before. It was an enraged roar.

She opened her eyes and growled as the pile of council lions bowled into Ronin. It was a massacre. No honor. No honor. Old Tarians had no honor.

She dug her claws into the ground and blasted toward them. Three steps. Three steps and then something barreled into her side like a missile. Fury smelled him before she hit the ground—Derek. He was Changed into his lion and was on her before she could get back up. Pain roared through her shoulder as he sank his teeth into her. She reached up and wrapped her arms around him, dug her claws in as hard as she could and raked them down his ribs. He released her and twisted, trying to avoid her weapons, but she wasn't fuckin' done. Up again, she leapt at him, scuffled and swatted, took her own licks, but he was on the defense now, backing up, looking confused. What, asshole, you thought I would just roll over and die?

Oh, God, she was present. Emerald was present. She had some control over this body for the first time in her life. Fury was letting her be here. She wanted to cry and scream and rejoice and rage. She didn't back off an inch, just hissed and clawed, and the second Derek gave her his back, she jumped on him and sank her teeth deep into the nape of his neck. Fuck the mane. It didn't faze her, and it sure as hell wouldn't protect him.

Look what you did, Derek. Look what you did.

Ronin. She needed to get to Ronin. Needed to help him. She used the vision of her father being dragged behind Derek's snowmobile to fuel her. The snap of his spine echoed through her like a gunshot. And in the moments she laid over him, teeth clamped on her kill, she searched but found no guilt.

Over his limp body, she zeroed in on the other side of the clearing. Pairs of lions were fighting, but through the battles, she could see Ronin, fighting and clawing his way at every lion within arm's length. There were bodies in the snow around him, and his coat was streaked with crimson. Every muscle rippled as he turned and went after another. The council was being wary. Probably best, because

Ronin looked like a monster. He wasn't even playing defense. He was actively attacking the lions around him.

There were still too many, though. Which one was Cassius? Was he one of the lifeless lions on the ground?

She released Derek and ran for Ronin. *I'm coming, just hold on!*

Three lions were on him now, and more were coming for him. She was going to make it. She would get to him. Just protect your neck! If she could just get to him, no one would have a shot at his throat. She would maim anyone who tried. King. Alpha. Her mate. Mine. Fury saw his lion and that was it. He was hers.

She dodged a fight, and then another. One of the lions clipped her leg out from under her as she passed, but she recovered before she went down completely. Heart pounding, she pushed her body faster. It wasn't until the last possible second that she saw Cassius on her. He was already airborne, arms outstretched, eyes intent on her, claws extended. She tried to duck him, but it was too late. She hit the ground like she'd fallen from a skyscraper and the air whooshed out of her lungs. She writhed in the cold snow, trying to see straight enough to fight back, but she felt claws on her flank immediately. No, no, no! Struggling to drag a breath, she pushed up and time slowed to a crawl. Fifteen yards away, Ronin was under a pile of massive lions, lashing out and biting, showing no fear in his furious glowing eyes. The lions around her were killing each other. There was no help for Ronin, and above her, Cassius had one powerful arm raised, his two-inch claws extended as the death blow came for her, the promise of pain in his gold eyes.

And this was the end. It wasn't fair. One day with Ronin wasn't enough. She'd waited her whole life for that day, and it wasn't *nearly* enough.

She closed her eyes just before Cassius's paw made contact with her face. She knew it would hurt bad, so she squeezed them closed as hard as she could. But as one second went by, then another, the blow never came. As she eased her eyes open again, she couldn't believe what she saw.

Cassius was covered in lionesses.

Just...covered.

Those submissive lionesses he'd been abusing

had risen up against him. Those meek little mice weren't mice anymore—they were motherfuckin' weapons.

The only thing she could hear was the snarling of the lionesses. The only part of him she could see were his eyes, locked on her, wide with fear. Fear. On Cassius.

Dragging in one shuddering breath, giving her lungs relief from the burn, she stood to run for Ronin, but above the snarling of the lionesses, something else terrifying rose from the woods. The roaring of bears.

Bears?

Ronin was standing against the horde now, but he wasn't alone anymore.

A scarred-up, black-maned lion was beside him, ears flattened against his head, lips curled back, exposing long teeth. Emerald would never forget the Reaper as long as she lived. She'd seen him when he was born into existence. The council had created him and then used him as their weapon. His empty eyes had visited her nightmares when she was younger, but now he was different. He was standing beside Ronin, daring the council to make a step toward them. This was the old enforcer of the Tarian Pride, here to back his best friend.

He and Ronin were the same size and had the same promise of pain etched into their monstrous faces. Behind them, more lions stalked forward, and then three massive she-grizzlies charged from the woods, skidding to a stop beside the Alphas.

Holy. Fuck.

If the Grim Reaper had come to aid Ronin, that meant these were his people—the Daughters of Beasts.

The New Tarian Pride had been so colossally outnumbered by the Old Tarian Pride, their allies, and the council...but Ronin had allies of his own.

As the Old Tarian Pride aimed for Ronin and the Daughters of Beasts, a freckled woman stepped from the shadows, her dark hair whipping in the wind as she lifted her hand. Her face transformed into a snarl as she flicked her fingers, and one of the charging lions was thrown to the side, slamming into a tree with a deafening crack. Lightning struck all around the clearing, illuminating everyone, lifting all of Emerald's fur with static. Witch.

Behind them, a trail of fire blew from the sky,

illuminating the underbelly of a dragon. Fiery red scales, and holy fuck...Vyr Daye was here.

Emerald closed the distance between her and Ronin, but he didn't need her protection. The hurricane wind from the dragon's wings was scattering the attackers. All around her, lions were crouching, slinking off toward the woods, hissing, tails down. The lionesses were hunkered down, but they weren't running. Beautiful badasses.

Pride surged through her as she watched the Old Tarians fleeing. As she watched the council scattering like roaches.

How could they ever look strong after this?

How could they ever truly rebuild after this?

Cassius had murmured those awful words as he'd left her room. *I win.*

But as she ran her face down the side of Ronin's tattered one, she knew Cassius had been wrong. Ronin was alive. He was still strong, bloodied and battered perhaps, but not even swaying or favoring injuries.

He leaned into her touch and then nudged her behind him. He filled the night air with something she hadn't even been able to imagine. A victory roar over the Old Tarians.

And the Reaper and the Daughters of Beasts answered.

And the surviving New Tarians answered.

And the lionesses answered.

The dragon answered.

And Fury...well...she answered, too.

He'd come for her. He hadn't left her, hadn't abandoned her to fight what was happening on her own. He'd come here tonight, right in the middle of the new council rising to power, and changed the course of this Pride's destiny.

Ronin wasn't just the Alpha of the *New* Tarians anymore.

He was the true Tarian Alpha.

And Emerald had never been prouder to be a part of something.

She'd never been proud of being born a Tarian before, but in this moment, as she lifted her own roar with the others...she was.

Everything was different now.

FOURTEEN

"Are you all okay?" she asked the women sitting around the living room.

"No," Sora said, her bottom lip quivering with the admission. She cradled her warm mug of hot cocoa closer and tried to smile at Emerald. "But we will be."

Emerald perched on the arm of the couch and looked around. Two hours ago, this cabin's furniture had been covered with sheets. This place hadn't been lived in since the Pride split. "You know you don't have to stay in this place. It's not girls vs. boys like the other Pride. You can all live where you're comfortable. Rose even lives outside of the territory line, if any of you ever wanted to live in town or anything."

"Why are you telling us this?" Annamora asked. "Does Ronin not want us here?"

"Ronin most certainly wants you here," he rumbled from the open doorway.

Orion stepped out of the way to let him pass, exposing his neck. Ronin clapped him on the shoulder. "You look like hell, man."

Indeed, Orion was sliced and diced from claw marks. He'd gone to war right alongside his sister, Sora, and the lionesses. "Speak for yourself," he said, wincing. "You look like hamburger."

Ronin laughed. "I fuckin' feel like it."

Ronin was a sight for sore eyes. Emerald hadn't seen him in a couple hours, not since they'd all come back to the territory. She'd missed him. Sitting next to him in his truck on the drive back, his hand on her leg, her holding onto his arm for dear life as they stared ahead silently in shock, hadn't been enough time for her to truly feel safe again. And Ronin was safety.

Now, it was all sinking in. They were okay.

He pulled up a chair right next to where she sat on the arm of the couch and brushed his fingertips across her knee before he spoke. "You're all welcome here. I can't imagine what you went through, but I saw you all tonight, and you protected Emerald. In a way, you protected me." He shook his head slightly. "I don't even know you, but I was so damn proud. This isn't like the other Pride, though. You can choose to stay and pledge to my Pride, or you can go anywhere you want. You. Aren't. Trapped. Not anymore."

Emerald swore she heard at least three sighs of relief.

Annamora looked at Ronin's hand on Emerald's leg. "You picked good." Her expression was raw and open, her eyes rimmed with tears when she looked up at Emerald. "You changed everything for us. You gave us some fight."

Emerald's voice would crack if she answered right away, so she swallowed a few times before she tried. "When I saw you girls on Cassius? Your lionesses? It was hands down the coolest moment of my life. You're submissive like me, and I know how hard it is to break a habit of fear, stick up for yourself, and just...let the animal have you. And you all did it tonight." Warmth streamed down her cheeks, but she didn't wipe the tears away. They could see her vulnerable. Tonight, these women had become her people. They'd had her back when it would've been easier to sit inside and stay safe until it was all over. "If you ever need anything, I'm your girl."

Annamora stood, lifted her chin proudly, and approached her and Ronin slowly. Then she looked at the other girls before she knelt. "Ronin, I pledge to you because I pledge to Emerald. I don't know you as an Alpha. But since the moment I met Emerald, my lioness *knew* her. She's different. She's a queen. And if she chooses you, I trust her. She wouldn't pick anyone who isn't a worthy king."

Emerald gasped as the other women fell to their knees. She didn't understand.

"Ronin?" she whispered, tears just streaming.

But he was smiling. Proudly. He pulled her against his ribs and kissed her temple. And she could feel it, how proud he was of her. That was a real man. That was love. When a man wasn't intimidated by a woman's power, but awed by it? That was strength.

She didn't know what the proper thing to do was, so she did what she wanted. What her lioness wanted. She needed affection, so she leaned in and kissed Ronin tenderly, gripping his shirt because this man had become so important. And then she fell to her knees in front of Annamora and hugged her. She buried her face against the woman's shoulder, and when she reached her arm out for Sora, they all piled on. She laughed as the girls hugged. Emerald stared at the ceiling fan, amazed at how anything could feel so good. Ronin's hands were on her shoulders; he was right behind her, always behind her. And the girls were going to be okay. She would make sure of it. Being a queen wasn't about being better than someone. Or being higher up. It wasn't about power. Not to Emerald. It was about making other women feel like queens, too. The broken and the kicked, those were her people. The ones who had nowhere to go but up. She'd been there. She'd been sitting on rock bottom waiting for someone to save her, but she hadn't known she didn't need someone to save her. She'd just needed Ronin to show her that she could save herself.

And because of that? He would always have her loyalty and the loyalty of Fury. Someday, she was going to explain that to him, but for now, she was going to enjoy the climb. She was going to enjoy the life she would build with him. And build, she would. She'd believed once that she'd been destined for no special fate. But as she looked over her shoulder at her man, cut up and exhausted from defending her, she knew she'd been wrong.

Her destiny was to protect the neck of the Tarian Alpha.

And he would protect hers in return.

FIFTEEN

His hand around hers felt like a big moment. He was leading her through the snow toward the big house, but with his hand, his cut, calloused, strong hand, clasped around hers...Emerald hadn't realized life could be like this.

He turned and smiled. The man bore claw marks on every inch of his body, but he still smiled at her. When he saw her face, though, he stopped and turned, cupped her cheeks. "What's wrong, Sweet Kitty."

"I'm just overwhelmed."

He searched her face, worry swimming in his eyes. "Did they hurt you?"

Her lip trembled. and she rubbed her cheek

against his palm, cupping it with her own hand to keep him touching her. "No. I don't think they could if they tried. I think when I saw Derek dragging my dad behind that snowmobile..."

"No one will ever hurt you or your dad again." He rumbled, "Look at me."

She lifted her gaze and gripped the hem of his shirt. It was just them, alone on the trail between the big cabin and where the girls were settling in for the night.

"No one." He shook his head slowly, and his eyes morphed from blue to that stunning green-gold. "When I saw you running for that snowmobile, for Derek, I was scared for the first time in as long as I can remember. I was scared you would get hurt. And then I watched you beat the ever-loving shit out of his face, watched his shock. I wanted to get to you, but more than that, I was so fucking happy you did that to him. Your protective instinct is so sexy, Em." When he pulled her close, she could feel it against her cheek—his steady heartbeat. "And then I saw your lioness fight Derek tonight. I could tell you were trying to get to me. Every time I looked over at you, at your lioness posted up, not afraid a bit, smaller than him but going for that neck, going for a kill shot...I don't think I've ever been prouder of a person in all my life. You were beautiful, Em. You know that, right? You were lethal grace, relentless. He didn't make you cower a bit. Big old dominant lion and look what you did. You know how strong you are, right?"

"I just learned tonight," she whispered thickly.

"It's just the beginning. Those women in there are on a completely different path because you gave them confidence and empowered them. What better queen could there be?"

"Ronin?"

"Yeah?" he asked, resting his forehead on hers.

"I don't want you to choose me because they follow me. I want you to choose me because of me."

"Silly, Sweet Kitty. I watched you when I was a boy. Wished for you. Wished for someday. It took us a lifetime, but we found that someday. You could've stayed submissive and quiet, and I would've still burned all of those pairing contracts. I wanted you either way. There was always something about you. When you wouldn't answer my texts? I went insane with worry. And then your dad woke up and told me about the murmurings he'd heard about the revival of the council, and I couldn't wait. I had to trust you to handle yourself, yeah, but I also had to trust what you'd told me. To believe in my Pride and give them a chance to prove themselves." He gripped her hair and rubbed his forehead against hers. "And you were right. You. Fixed. Everything that was broken. That's power, Em. When you see something and call it out, dig in, support change, that's power. You did that, not knowing if you would ever see me or my Pride again. You did it for me. I couldn't respect another person any more than I do you. The lionesses pledging their fealty to the Pride? That's a bonus. I was already with you before tonight, though."

She rolled her eyes closed and sighed in relief. Slipping her hands around his shoulders, she hugged him up tight. Ronin was purring. Purring! Big old beat-up Alpha, and he purred at her touch.

This was really happening. To her.

"Come on," he murmured. He kissed her sweetly and then pulled her by the hand again toward the big cabin. "I have someone who has been clawing at the walls to see you safe."

Emerald followed him through the back door of the cabin, down the hallway, and into a room. God, if felt like a hundred years had passed between now and the time she'd seen her dad's lifeless body in the snow.

Rose was sitting on the edge of his bed with a bowl of steaming soup, talking low to Dad. When the silver-haired woman looked up, her cheeks were flushed. She made her way out, but Emerald didn't miss it. The woman's smile stayed on her lips the entire time.

"You look much better than the last time I saw you," she said, making her way to the bed.

Dad's dark eyebrows lifted as he ran his hand through his silver hair and exposed a long row of stitches. Stitches on a lion shifter with heightened healing meant someone had bashed his head in pretty good. "I feel much better. Those Old Tarians aren't very hospitable."

"Yeah, well..." Emerald cast a glance back at Ronin, standing in the open doorway with his arms crossed over his chest. "The New Tarians are different. Thank God." She inhaled deeply and said, "I was really scared you were dead."

"It's okay," he said suddenly.

She didn't understand what he meant, though.

"What's okay?"

"Staying here. You don't have to run anymore if you don't want to." He cast a quick glance at Ronin. "I like him."

"I'll give you some space," Ronin murmured. He nodded respectfully. "Sir."

Dad watched him go and then wrapped Emerald's hand in his own. "It's not like it used to be here. Not anymore. I believe in that one. Ronin. He was just as worried about you as I was."

"Whatever," she whispered. "I saw you checking out Rose's butt when she walked away. That's the real reason you want to stay."

Dad shrugged and offered her a remorseless smirk, the silver fox. "Well, she ain't hard on the eyes."

"Oh, my God." She waved her hand in the air. "I'm glad you are alive, but I'm not having discussions about your lady friends."

"Lady friends?" Dad scrunched up his face. "How old do you think I am?"

"Like four hundred and sixteen years old."

Dad's face went comically blank. "You're grounded."

Emerald giggled. God, she was so happy he was okay. They could've so easily missed this moment. Both of them had been in the heart of the Old Tarian Pride, the most lethal Pride of lion shifters in the world, and look where they'd ended up. Joking in Ronin's room, her dad tucked in bed with soup still steaming on the nightstand, a fire in the hearth nearby, and an entire Pride outside that would keep them safe.

"I like him, too," she whispered, eyes on the thread she was picking at on the comforter.

"Ronin?"

She nodded.

"Baby, you always did. He's the only one I've ever heard you talk about. Hey," he murmured, stilling her hand from plucking at the thread. "It's okay to let yourself care. I did with your mom, and it was the best decision I ever made. It's what I want for you, too."

Her dad's blessing meant the world to her. He had been her rock for so long, and she trusted him. He was giving his approval, and she wanted to start crying all over again. No one person deserved to be this happy, right? It probably messed with the cosmic balance or something—this much happiness inside of one person.

But then again, who was she to question what was happening? Her dad seemed relaxed for the first time in years, and Ronin's last kiss still tingled on her lips, filling all the holes that had been in her heart before him.

It was okay to be happy. To fight for something she wanted. For a life she wanted.

"I want to stay," she whispered.

Dad's smile was easy and steady, and his dark eyes danced. "That's what I hoped you would say."

SIXTEEN

The day had been eternal.

It was four in the morning, and down to her bones, Emerald was exhausted. She'd stayed up late talking to her dad and then stumbled out into the hallway to find voices echoing from the kitchen.

She couldn't help the smile on her face when she saw everyone. The Pride was still awake— Kannon and Terrence and Gray were here. The Daughters of Beasts were also here with Grim, the Red Dragon, Vyr, and his mate Riyah. They were all wearing PJs and gathered around the kitchen island. Ronin wore no shirt, but she couldn't even be that big of a perv because he was covered in bandages. Low-slung gray sweats hung from his hips, and his hair was all mussed like he'd rubbed his hand through it a bunch.

And even though his eyes were tired, his smile was megawatt when he saw her. "There she is," he murmured. "Come here. I want you to meet some friends."

His arm was outstretched, and sleepily, she slipped against his side and rested her cheek on his shoulder. "I'm Emerald," she introduced herself.

The others introduced themselves, too, and when it came to Grim, he said, "Hey, I remember you."

"I remember you, too, but you're really different," she murmured. "The last time I saw you, the Reaper was new. And terrifying."

"Yeah," Kannon said, spinning a half-full beer slowly in his fingertips, "He's still terrifying."

"At least you're on his good side," Ronin murmured.

One of Grim's Crewmates, Rhett, leaned toward Kannon and said with a mischievous wink, "Might want to keep it that way."

Ronin pulled up a bar stool and settled Emerald onto it before he stroked his fingers lightly down her spine and said, "I have to ask, Vyr. Why did you come?"

The red-haired man took a long swig of his beer and murmured, "My son is a Tarian lion. I don't want him to grow up ashamed of where he came from. If the council was revived with Cassius as Alpha, and the Tarian Pride went back to their old ways, how could he not be ashamed? I want better for my boy. Ronin, I believe you can fix this Pride." Vyr shrugged. "And if you can't, then I'll just burn you and devour your ashes."

"Hmm," Ronin said, nodding.

Vyr winked at Emerald and took another sip of his beer, but she was still about thirty-four percent disturbed. She'd seen his dragon on the news and believed he was fully capable of following through with that threat. He would have to go through her, though.

They stayed up for a little while, but eventually, the Pride started trickling away, and the girls in the Daughters of Beasts crew nodded off on the couch. And before she knew it, Ronin was carrying her to his room.

"What happened?" she asked softly.

"You fell asleep. It was cute," he assured her.

Well, thank goodness for small blessings because

sometimes she snored when she was exhausted, and that would've been truly embarrassing if she'd—"

"You were snoring."

Oh, God.

He shut his door behind her and settled her on the bed, pulled back the covers, and tucked her in as she got comfortable and made a pillow nest. He made his way to the same chair he'd sat in when she'd awoken here a few days ago.

"Nope," she said, shaking her head. "Come sleep here." Emerald lifted the corner of the blanket invitingly.

"You've been through a lot, Em."

"Being close to you makes me feel safe."

The sound in his throat was positively satisfied, and he climbed in bed with her, scooped her into his arms, and pulled her against his strong chest. If his injuries hurt, he didn't act like it. Perhaps he was simply too tired to react to pain right now.

He pressed his nose against her hair and inhaled deeply, and she understood. She was taking comfort from his scent, too. And his warmth. And the beating of his heart, and the feel of his skin against hers. Desperate to be closer, she peeled her sweater off and then her jeans, too. Ronin's hand went to her waist and gripped her hard, and she rocked against his hips. His dick was hard and swollen behind the thin material of his sweats. Even those were too much of a barrier right now, so she hooked her fingers in the elastic band and tugged them downward. She giggled as he kicked out of them. Was she delirious with exhaustion? Was that why she was laughing during intimacy? Or was she just that comfortable with him already?

Ronin shoved her panties down her thighs as he smiled against her lips, chuckling into their kiss. Good gah, he was so sexy. She ran her fingertips through his hair as he rocked against her, hitting her just right with his thick shaft. She arched her back and moaned, sliding her leg over his, opening up the apex between her thighs.

Her body had been sore and injured and tired a few minutes ago, but now it was ready to go, growing wetter by the second with every pump of his body against hers. She could come just like this with him rubbing her, but she wanted more. Needed more. After everything that had happened, she needed him to make her feel like she was his, soul and body.

He took his time, trailing his hand down her arm, then down the side of her breast to her waist. He traced the curve of her ass and then up to her hair. He gripped it in the back and turned her head when she purred. Lips near her ear, he whispered, "I choose you."

Emerald rolled her eyes closed at how good those words made her heart feel. He chose her. Really chose her. He was giving her a place beside him, under his protective wing, where she would defend him always.

There was something so freeing about being confident in your place in the world. And for the first time in her life, she knew her place. It was here with Ronin. Her Ronin.

His lips pressed to hers, and she reveled in the taste of her mate. Because even though they hadn't said that word, that's what they were. No contract could hold a candle to what they felt or the bond they'd already created.

She'd found him—her person. Her other half.

Ronin's hand left her hair and gripped the back of her neck as he rolled on top of her. He was heavy, solid, like a weighted blanket. Safe, safe, safe. He pushed her knees apart, and she begged. What else could she do? Her mind was gone now, off in the sky somewhere while her body just felt, and did, and reacted to its other half. He pressed the swollen head of his cock into her entrance just enough for her to bow against the bed. She whispered another aching plea, "Please, Ronin. Deeper."

Their bodies moved like waves rolling against each other. Like they'd been doing this dance for eons and knew exactly what the other needed. She slid her hands up his back as he settled firmly between her legs, and then he was there, sliding into her. Deeper...deeper. Emerald couldn't help the needy noises she made, but from the hungry look in his eyes, they were just fine with Ronin. His hands were everywhere and they were fire, burning trails of ecstasy up and down her skin. And when his lips drifted from her mouth to her neck, down, down to her breast, then plucking gently at her nipple, she lost it. Eyes closed to the world, she let herself drown in him. She didn't exist, and Ronin didn't exist. They only existed as one now. He stayed deep in her for a few moments, and she reveled in the sensation of being filled with him. Moving slowly, Ronin drew rapture from her, teasing with his lips, tempting her with his touch, until her entire body craved him. Every nerve ending adored him. Every sigh from her lips drew a slight curve of his. Oh, that man knew he had her. He was playing her like some string instrument he'd practiced his whole life.

He moved in her smoothly, sure to hit her clit and hold it every thrust. Sliding his hands up her forearms, he pinned her hands above her head and kissed her. His tongue stroked into her mouth with the same rhythm that his dick was sliding into her. Slow and controlled at first, and then he slipped little by little as the growl in his throat grew louder. His cock filled her over and over until she was writhing against him. And when at last she lost all sense of control and begged him, "Faster," he slammed into her and held. Slammed, held, faster. Faster. Faster. "Right there," she whispered, holding his hands as he intertwined their fingers above her head.

Ronin grunted, spread his knees wider and went even deeper, bucking into her hard. Oh, she was there, she was there! Her body pulsed hard, gripping his dick. His body was so tense as he rammed into her and held, his dick swelling and releasing, erupting inside of her until she was filled with warmth. He moved with her until they were both spent. And then he rolled her over on her side and hugged her close, kissing her like she mattered. And she did matter.

I choose you.

She smiled in the dark, in the arms of the man she loved. In the embrace of her future. And she whispered the words she never thought a simple girl like her was destined to say. "I choose you back."

She'd learned big lessons. She'd thought her life wasn't her choice, but there was always a choice. The only person who could ever tether her to a dark future was her. She'd just had to become brave enough to take a leap of faith and trust in the man who'd saved her from a bully all those years ago. Who had protected her from an entire Pride today.

Her new life wasn't all tied up in a pretty package with a perfect bow. Some of the council had escaped. Some of the Old Tarians had escaped. The girls here would need help to rehabilitate and gain confidence, and Ronin would have a long and bumpy road ahead as he would fight to maintain one of the biggest lion Prides in existence. Not every day would be a rainbow, but enough of them would. And as long as the good days existed, well…then the bad ones would be okay, too.

The most important part was that she wasn't alone, and her mate, her Alpha, her Ronin…he would never be alone again either.

From this day on…she would be a proud Tarian lioness.

From this hour on…there would be no more running.

From this moment on…home became a person.

Home was Ronin.

Want more of these characters?

The New Tarian Pride series is a standalone series set in the Damon's Mountains Universe.
More of these characters can be found in the following series:

Saw Bears

Gray Back Bears

Fire Bears

Boarlander Bears

Harper's Mountains

Kane's Mountains

Red Havoc Panthers

Sons of Beasts

Daughters of Beasts

About the Author

T.S. Joyce is devoted to bringing hot shifter romances to readers. Hungry alpha males are her calling card, and the wilder the men, the more she'll make them pour their hearts out. She werebear swears there'll be no swooning heroines in her books. It takes tough-as-nails women to handle her shifters.

She lives in a tiny town, outside of a tiny city, and devotes her life to writing big stories. Foodie, wolf whisperer, ninja, thief of tiny bottles of awesome smelling hotel shampoo, nap connoisseur, movie fanatic, and zombie slayer, and most of this bio is true.

Bear Shifters? Check

Smoldering Alpha Hotness? Double Check

Sexy Scenes? Fasten up your girdles, ladies and gents, it's gonna to be a wild ride.

> For more information on T. S. Joyce's work,
> visit her website at
> www.tsjoyce.com

Printed in Great Britain
by Amazon